Wit

winning novelist, Ron Butlin is also a former
F ' ' ' ' et-Laureate. He has   lished
            books. B   a
            a

barnacle-scraper on the River Thames and a
male model. Widely translated, his work has
twice been awarded a Best Foreign Novel
prize. He lives in Edinburgh with his wife,
the writer Regi Claire, and their dog.

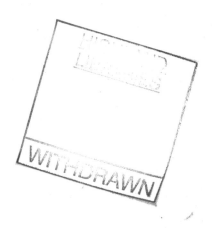

STEVE & FRANDAN

TAKE ON THE WORLD

RON BUTLIN

First published in 2017 by
BC Books, an imprint of
Birlinn Limited
West Newington House
10 Newington Road
Edinburgh
EH9 1QS

www.bcbooksforkids.co.uk

ISBN 978 1 78027 439 3
British Library Cataloguing-in-Publication Data
A catalogue record for this book is available from the British Library

Designed by James Hutcheson
Typeset by Initial Typesetting Services, Edinburgh
Printed and bound by Grafica Veneta

I

Steve's in a hurry – a real hurry. But halfway down the street he is stopped by his next-door neighbour. Mr Connor is sounding off as usual. Talk-talk-talk – same old, same old, and spit-spraying like a monsoon. If Steve was in charge there'd be no Connors allowed on his street, on the planet even.

He stares up at the spittle-wet lips, the mile-long nose hairs waving in the breeze, the stuck-on eyes. What kind of a kid grows up into a *Connor*?

Steve tunes in for a moment –

'... can't fool me, nobody in this town can, so let me tell you ...'

– and tunes out again.

How long's this going to go on for? He needs to move-move-move. Fran's been texting him every five minutes to get his ass in gear.

But wait up – the monsoon has eased, and Connor's wandering off to find someone else to hassle.

Steve texts back to Fran – *See u in 5* ☺ – then blasts off down the street.

Taking every backstreet and shortcut in town, clambering over walls, dodging between parked cars behind the supermarket and sprinting through the graveyard at full speed, Steve keeps his head down. For the last fortnight he and Dan have had to stay off the main streets. School's been a nightmare, and out of school even worse. The sooner they get away from here the better.

The river looks calm, not a ripple in sight. No one about, thank goodness. Here's hoping it stays that way. A few ducks are paddling around in circles and someone's walking their dog on the opposite bank, and that's it. Couldn't be better.

He pulls off his trainers and Simpsons socks and stacks them under the bush next to where they've hidden their stores. For the last week they've been sneaking tins of meat, baked beans and spaghetti hoops from their homes, as well as biscuits, chocolate and large bottles of cola. A little at a time so no one will notice, said Fran. They'll need all they can get because there'll be no

McDonald's where they're going, no Burger Kings – with any luck, no civilisation at all.

The reeds have grown so tall at this bend that a kind of secret harbour's been formed. It's completely hidden, which is exactly what they needed.

Steve shouts across, 'How's it going?'

'Be a lot faster now you're here,' Fran's voice comes back to him from behind the reeds.

'Too right,' adds Dan.

Steve steps down into the river, sinking into the muddy ooze at the bottom. It's like brown smoke curling up between his toes and clouding over his feet. *Splash! Splash! Splash!* He pushes through the screen of reeds to where the FranDan twins are securing an oil drum into position. The two of them are standing knee-deep in the water; Fran's rolled up her jeans, Dan hasn't bothered or else forgot. The drum's bright red, but it can't be helped.

The raft's looking good. It'll get them out of here, which it has to ASAP – another week like the last two and they're likely to crack up. Dan will for sure. Helping build the raft and stealing food for their hoard is all that's kept him going. That, and knowing that they'll soon be far away from Thor and his Vikings.

It's taken them a week to construct the raft. Floor-boards from their soon-to-be-demolished old primary school, empty oil drums from the forecourt of the FranDan garage (for a school project, they told their dad), and a clothes line somebody donated without even needing asked. Mrs Connor, in fact. Mr Connor might be a seriously weird piece of broken-down clockwork, but his wife's cool – she lives on Planet Happy and you can often hear her rhyming and singsong-ing herself up and down the street.

Steve clambers on board in time to help with securing the oil drum. Fran gives her twin brother, Dan, one end of a length of rope to loop round and round the nail he's hammered into the end of a plank. Dan then passes the rope back to Steve. Even though the deck still dips into the water now and again, depending on how they shift about on it, the three of them are agreed that every oil drum lashed into position makes the raft feel that bit more stable. It's going to be top of the range. A real eco-craft – no engine, powered by paddles and river current only. Totally silent, like *they*'ll be. Invisible, a stealth raft travelling by night, under everyone's radar. When all the drums are fixed in place, the wooden planks won't be getting wet any more, but riding high above the waterline – and with the three of them on top!

'Almost done,' says Fran. She's the leader of the twins – popped out first and never lets Dan forget it. She takes the rope end from Steve and pulls it tight before hitching it firmly to the underside of the plank. There's enough room for their stores and to let them all lie down at the same time, though they'll be taking turns to keep watch as they drift through the darkness. As well as a clothes pole (thanks again to Mrs Connor) for shoving themselves away from the bank, they're bringing a tent for when it rains. This time tomorrow they'll be sailing downstream on their very own state-of-the-art, all-weather raft.

Then Fran says the magic words. 'We managed to get another couple of drums this afternoon. And so ... we can leave *tonight!*'

Big grins, whoops all round, cries of 'YES!' and high fives.

Work on the extra drums takes them another hour. The raft's looking awesome! The deck's now a good three inches above the waterline and they'd have to be really stupid to capsize it. Which they're not, so they won't. They'll cast off at midnight, and Steve's to bring his dad's wind-up torch. More grins and more high fives. YES! YES! YES!

Once Steve gets home, he'll have his dinner – Tuesday means pizza – and hang around to watch some crap on TV with his mum and dad so everything looks normal. At the usual time he'll say goodnight and go up to his room. Making no noise, he'll get himself packed. Then, just before midnight, he'll tiptoe down the stairs and slip out the back door. He can hardly wait.

'See you soon!' he calls back to FranDan and shoots off up the road. A few minutes later he's about to take the shortcut through the cemetery when he hears someone shouting behind him.

'There's one of them!'

He starts to run. If he goes fast enough he'll reach home in ten. Just as well Nessie's not with him or she'd be hanging back hoping for biscuits or chocolate. They're bullies, but if they ever try to touch Nessie he'll stomp them.

'Picking out your gravestone, are you?' shouts one of them.

'Maybe you and Dan can share a grave?' yells another.

'Cheaper all round!' a third joins in.

He recognises their voices. Half-Pint, a squashed elf who stopped growing before ever getting started, with Big Robo and Pizza McBride.

Maybe he should let them catch up, then thump the three of them? Half-Pint'll be the same as swatting a fly and Big Robo's got so few brain cells he'll be on the ground before he notices he's been knocked down. And as for Pizza McBride, he's all dough with nothing on top.

Steve's about to turn round and deal with them when he hears more voices. A lot more. Half a dozen at least.

So no turning back to thump anyone. He picks up speed and races for home.

Steve is Mr Perfect all evening. They eat pizza and salad, plates on their laps, his mum and dad on the couch and him on the floor with his back against the armchair and his legs stretched full out. Nessie keeps herself beside him – with a dog like her you never eat alone. It's a double-cheese meat feast, two for one because today's Tuesday. On his planet every day would be a Tuesday. Tomorrow night they might be eating fish out the river, or maybe rabbits – and no salad. Definitely no salad.

He's put his phone on silent, so if FranDan call his parents won't start asking questions – parents need to be protected.

'Don't bolt your food, Steve, there's plenty more,' says his mother, not taking her eyes from the television. A dozen muscled policemen, the writing on their jerseys and helmets in a foreign language Steve doesn't recognise, are shouting at hundreds and hundreds of people, some of them carrying kids and rucksacks, some of them plastic supermarket bags, and some carrying nothing at all, like they're out for a walk. The people are shouting back. A woman lifts up her wee toddler into a cop's face. They're dressed the same as anyone from round here; and they look the same as anyone from round here. The cop's eyes go like Connor's and you can see he'd like to stomp her with all he's got, but knows he's on camera. The world's looking at him; Steve and his parents are looking at him. The boy's started to cry, he's so far from his home and so lost that he—

Steve's mobile vibrates. A text. He sneaks a quick peek. Fran: *More food. Tin opener?*

'That's just along from where we were on holiday a couple of years back – had a great beach and everything,' says his dad before upending his can for a couple of last chugs. 'What's the world coming to?'

'It's your world,' Steve says, before he can stop himself. His mobile vibrates again.

'Don't start all that again.' There's the hiss of another can being opened. His dad does it one-handed, which is cool if you like that kind of thing. Dan and Steve tried some beer once – tasted like battery fluid, fizzed up. Steve takes a sip of coke and reaches for another slice. Still three left. He's going to miss Tuesdays. Soon his dad'll be snoring through Celebrity Big Brother like a whale on steroids. But by then he'll be upstairs packing the last of his things.

One slice left now – his. Well, his and Nessie's. Then he's out of here.

Standing in the hall, Steve checks his texts to make sure no one's bottled out at the last minute. 'No one' meaning Dan.

It's from Fran. *Remember – no mobile. No mobile = no Thor. See u soon :-)*

No Thor sounds good. A cold sweat runs down Steve's back. Ice-sweat, but the rest of him's burning. Burning angry.

Not so sure about leaving his mobile at home though. He can see why, of course, but . . .

He texts back: *OK. See u at 00.00.*

Nearly quarter to midnight. Spare socks and underwear, sweater and jeans, sleeping bag in his backpack and Steve's good to go. He reads through the letter he's leaving his parents. It's taken him ages, like writing something for school but much harder. Having written it again and again to get it right means it's really late now and he has to leave. Lucky there's plenty of phrases he hears them say all the time, and he's used them. It sounds good – the best he can do, anyway. He's not said how bad everything is. Just couldn't.

Dear Mum and Dad,

Everything's fine. I am fine. Really. Me and FranDan are taking time out for a few days. We need to. Some R&R. Feeling stressed and need some space. Too much pressure. I will be back. I promise. DON'T WORRY. Everything's fine. Really.

Love, Steve

Then he texts FranDan: *On my way.*

One part of him's already out of the front door, through the town and down the river, paddling the raft at full speed and making it skim over the water like a hoverboard. The other part's still standing there, like he's taking in his room for the very first time, the outline of his bed that he's slept in every night of his life, apart from holidays.

His room equals his life equals *him*.

Is that what he'll be closing the door on? Himself? And for good? He wants to go, and he doesn't want to go. Thor – that cyber-slimebag!

Phone's vibrating: Fran texting *Move it!* But she's added a ☺.

OK.

How could he leave his mobile? Easy said, not so easy done. His mobile's like his room, it's *him*.

Next moment, it's like he's watching his hand all by itself, sliding his mobile into his pocket.

He pulls on his backpack, eases his bedroom door slowly-slowly shut and tiptoes past his mum and dad's room. Their snoring's started. His like a backwards fart and hers like a bird that's not quite making it into song.

He creeps downstairs, keeping clear of every step that's got even the slightest creak-squeak. Waiting at the bottom is Nessie. She raises her head and looks him right in the eye. *Where are you going? Because I'm coming too.*

No way, he shakes his head, then lifts up the flap of her ear and whispers the magic word – *biscuits!* She follows him into the kitchen. When she's giving her full attention to a handful of crackers, he places his letter on the table for them to find in the morning then grabs some more tins out the cupboard. Tin opener? In the big drawer maybe? A rattle of ladles, big spoons, carving

knife, bread knife, cheese grater, things and more things –
everything but a tin opener and it's getting later and later.
The other drawer? No tin opener there either. Tins and
no opener? Fran'll have found one, bound to. She's Fran,
isn't she? He slips out the back door.

Except that once he reaches the street, he sees Nessie
has slipped out with him. She's looking up at him, eyes
bright and tail wagging: *Now what?*

If he goes back and tries shoving her indoors again,
she'll start barking. Nessie doesn't argue – she barks.
Which means she always wins. And if he runs fast,
trying to leave her behind, she'll run faster. So that's that.
Nessie's coming along too.

2

After switching off her mobile and sticking it at the back of her T-shirt and jersey drawer, Fran leaves her room. She closes the door quietly then goes along to the kitchen where Dan's waiting for her, backpack on.

'We won't be able to lock up properly after we—'

She puts her fingers to her lips. 'Shh! Got to be quiet.'

Dan nods. 'Sorry.'

'Shh, I said!'

They pass through the small shop at the side of the house, feeling their way as best they can by the hazy light from a faraway streetlamp and making sure not to bump into the counter and the revolving magazine stand immediately inside the shop entrance. Finally they step outside. As they pull the door behind them they hear the Yale lock click shut. The after-hours garage is in darkness: the line of petrol pumps unlit, the street silent and deserted.

That's it. They've left home now. No going back.

The forecourt's suddenly a dazzle of harsh brightness – Dan's set off the security light. 'Keep going,' hisses Fran. 'Cats are always tripping the beam at night.'

After a few minutes' walking, the two of them have turned off the empty main road and are heading down towards the river. They meet no one. To their left they can hear the faint rumble of heavy lorries on the bypass and the dual carriageway beyond. After two streets of parked cars and curtained windows, they come to their old primary school – now scheduled for demolition. Seen so near midnight, its broken windows, padlocked main door and wrought iron gate give it a haunted-house look.

Fran's already easing herself through a gap in the hoarding. 'We can cut across the playground. Much quicker.'

'Might be guard dogs.'

'Guarding what?' she calls back to him out of the darkness. 'Come on.'

Dan hurries after her. The river's at the back of the building, less than a minute away. As he crosses the deserted tarmac he speeds up, making it in record time.

Then they're over the wall, down the grass slope and through the trees.

And *there* it is.

Fran's proud of the raft – *her* raft. After all, *she* had the idea, *she* googled the instructions, *she* directed its construction – so it's hers really. Not that she calls it that when she's speaking to the boys, of course. Just before she steps onto it she glances round once more – by the faint light coming from the streetlamps on the riverbank she can see the outline of its six empty oil drums, one set in each corner plus one extra on each side, lashed to the wooden planks that form the deck. Underneath, the wood's lined with a sheet of tarpaulin from an old lorry so that no water comes up between the boards. Well, almost none anyway.

'Let's get loaded up,' she says. 'The moment Steve shows up, we're off!'

3

Steve and Nessie hurry through the deserted streets. Ever since the new bypass was opened a year ago the town's been shutting down, shops closing then standing empty, 'FOR SALE' signs up and down the high street. No through-traffic any more, no new people, only folk they've seen a million times before: there's the fat woman from the baker's; the shouting man from the super-market; the single traffic warden who has to wander round and round the same streets; local life forms like Connor; and the ancient hippie leftover from long before Steve and FranDan were born. You name them, they know them – and see them every single day. Tesco's finished off the small shops, and the only nightlife is two grim and windowless pubs. There's the one Steve's dad goes to and the other that everyone calls the Wild West because of the fights. As Steve goes past the Wild West he's watching out for drunks, especially aggro drunks – his dad gets sleepy-drunk, which is him at his best, totally out of it and no problem to anyone. After a few cans FranDan's dad morphs into an aggro drunk. Aggro with FranDan, aggro with their mum, with their cats even – Suki and Fudge often get themselves drop-kicked across the room just for sitting in his chair. He's got much worse recently, thanks to the bypass flushing his garage down the pan: hardly any breakdown work now and no passing trade for his pumps.

And that's how Thor, his Vikings and the rest of it all started.

It was when Dan turned up at school a month ago wearing new trainers. Nike? Reebok? Adidas? They were checked out. Blue Flash.

Blue Flash?

Then word got round. Blue Flash were Lidl's. One of that week's special offers. Less than a tenner. Dan was walking around in Blue Flash. The next week it was a Lidl T-shirt.

Then Thor posted on Facebook that anyone wearing Blue Flash dissed everyone who had to look at him.

A Viking posted a comment: *Anyone wearing Lidl has no life.*

Another Viking: *Anyone wearing Lidl is better off dead.*

Thor: *They should do everyone a favour and kill themselves.*

But Dan only had one pair of trainers. Blue Flash.

There were new postings every few minutes. Dozens of them. Dan was dissing everyone. Dan had no life, Dan was better off dead. Why didn't Dan go and kill himself?

Steve started posting dislikes. Sticking up for Dan. Sticking up for Blue Flash, sticking up for Lidl's. Saying that brands were just one big con trick, saying that Nike made labels, not trainers. It only made things worse.

More Thor posts, more Viking posts. Steve was palsy-walsy with Dan? Steve and Dan must be gay. Then their selfies were Photoshopped to look naked and gross and posted online. Steve and Dan should kill each other. Steve and Dan should double suicide. Time it for when Lidl has a special offer on coffins.

But what could they do? Thor and his Vikings were using fake accounts – no idea who they were but they had to be people in their school, in their class most likely.

23

Fran told them to ignore it, they were just creeps. 'Forget about them, they're not worth thinking about,' she said. Not so easy when it's all about you, though.

As Steve runs through the dark empty streets with Nessie bounding along beside him, excited to share in this late-night treat, he's picturing the raft and the three of them sailing off into the darkness, leaving Thor and his Vikings and the whole town itself far behind. He's also thinking about Fran. He likes Fran, likes her a lot.

But . . .

With her blonde hair and a smile he always thinks is just for him, he can't believe that Fran is in charge, but she is. She's an organiser, she organises everything, including him and Dan. He doesn't know how it happened or when it happened, but it just did. Leaving town was her idea, building the raft was her idea, leaving their mobiles behind was her idea. And so—

'Hey – Steve!'

He keeps going. It's Mr Norbett, aka No-brain, the handyman-joiner who helped his dad put in some kitchen stuff at home. Mr Norbett always talked with him when his dad wasn't there, asked what films he liked, if he read books and stuff, and told him how he should stick in at school and go to college, or he'd end up like him – end up like his dad, too, Mr Norbett meant, though he never said it. His dad called him No-brain because he was slow at measuring and working things out. Mr Norbett might be on Planet Slow, but he made their kitchen good as new.

'Steve!'

Mr Norbett's on the other side of the street. 'Hello, Mr Norbett. Sorry, can't stop to chat. Nessie got out and wandered off, and I'm taking her back home. In a real hurry now.'

'At this time of night? Your parents know you're out?'

'Yes. Bye!'

What else could he say?

'Home? But you're going the wrong way, Steve. Something the matter?' Mr Norbett starts across the street, clearly wanting to help, if he can. But Steve doesn't need help, doesn't want it.

'Nessie and me – we're late for …' Then he begins running. Nothing else for it. He can run a lot faster than

Mr Norbett – the old man's slow on his feet as well as in his head. Steve and Nessie hang a left down a side street with Mr Norbett trundling after them.

He picks up speed, his rucksack slap-slap-slapping against his back like it's urging him to go faster and faster, Nessie beside him running and wagging and wagging and running, thinking *what fun*, thinking *biscuits*.

He dashes across the small park, the old man trailing light years behind. Stopped altogether probably.

But because he's a really kind man, Mr Norbett will probably call his parents to let them know he's seen him. Steve doesn't need his kindness. Not just now.

Sharp left past the baker's and down the church lane.

Mr Norbett might not call them, of course. But if he does, the note Steve's left for his parents to find in the morning will be found far too soon, probably before they've even set off. Nothing else for it but to run faster. Midnight or not, he cuts through the graveyard – now he can really speed up, hopscotching from gravestone to gravestone, Nessie hopscotching beside him, loving it!

4

'Steve! At last!' calls Dan from the raft. 'Another minute and we'd have left without you. Hop aboard and let's go!' Then he sees Nessie. 'You've brought your dog?'

'She'll be our mascot,' says Fran. 'Good to have another girl on board. Anyway, every ship should have a ship's dog.'

'It's a ship's cat you're thinking of,' says Dan. 'For catching rats and—'

'No rats on our ship.' Steve steps on board. 'Nessie's going to be our guard dog, and we can send her ashore to hunt rabbits and stuff for dinner.' What he doesn't say is that she'll most likely eat anything she catches, eat it on the spot.

The raft feels good. Even with all three of them plus Nessie, their tent, sleeping bags and all their stores, it's hardly sunk an inch deeper into the water. Really solid. They take their positions. Steve at the back, ready to cast off, Dan sitting in the middle and holding Nessie so she doesn't jump around. Fran's at the front, clutching the Connor clothes pole. Just then, the clouds open and the moon comes out like it wants to show them the way. A good omen.

Speaking almost in a whisper, Steve counts out 'One, two, three!' and casts off. Fran pushes them away from the shore, then, once they're a few metres out, she puts down the pole and picks up the short piece of plank she's brought along to use as a paddle. Steve coils up the length of rope and sits down next to Nessie and Dan. Soon they're floating in midstream.

The river's about thirty metres across and very slow-moving, millpond calm.

They don't talk because their voices will carry over the still surface. The water ripples against the oil drums, a steady trickling sound, and they can feel a slight tug every so often as the raft shifts in the current.

Fran's on first watch. Sitting cross-legged at the front, she keeps totally rigid and upright, her eyes fixed straight ahead. Balanced across her knees is the homemade paddle to help steer whenever their course needs corrected. Beside her, the clothes pole's within reach ready to shove them clear of any rocks or if they find themselves getting too near the bank.

Almost soundlessly they drift through the rest of the town. Nessie's lying stretched out between the two boys; every so often she blinks her eyes then closes them again. Steve has his hand buried deep in her soft-fur warmth. The large stone buildings that loom up on either side like slabs of solid darkness gradually give way to open stretches and then, as they pass the playing fields, they see the white-painted goalposts shimmer like ghost-lines traced in the moonlight. Next, the tall chimney of McDowell's timber yard tells them they're near the very edge of town.

The moment Fran sees the chimney she knows the old bridge will be coming up after the next bend. She'd better get herself ready to paddle them clear. It has massive stone pillars set right in the middle of the river and if she's not careful—

'Fran!' she hears Steve whisper. 'The old bridge. We'll need to steer—'

'I know. We're fine,' she whispers back over her shoulder. 'Try to get to sleep. You'll be getting woken at

four to take your turn on watch. Dan first and then you, remember.'

Steve remembers all right, but *sleep?* Who can sleep? While the rest of the world is in bed, here's him and FranDan travelling alone through the darkness like they're the only people left on the planet, gliding along in silence under the brightest spread of stars he's ever seen, hundreds and hundreds of them.

A few moments later he feels the current speeding up, hears the trickling water sound getting louder. Beside him, Nessie's gone tense; she lifts her head and begins to make low growling noises in her throat.

All at once, they're really speeding up. Not far ahead he can hear the trickling sound change to a sudden gushing-rushing roar as the river divides to pass on either side of the main pillar. He straightens up. Nessie's on her haunches now and Dan's sitting up, too.

'What's happening?' asks Dan. 'What—'

'Quiet!' snaps Fran.

Ahead, they can hear the current smack into the solid stone, making a low rumble-tumble snarl as it swirls and churns in the darkness. The instant Steve gets to his feet, the raft tilts beneath him, washing water over the deck.

'Sit down!' Fran hisses. 'Don't move or we'll—' She breaks off and starts paddling furiously, stabbing the water. The current's rushing faster and faster. She paddles more and more fiercely but the raft's getting sucked nearer to the pillar. Steve grabs Nessie round the neck to keep her still, his hand holding her jaws shut to stop her from barking out loud.

THUD! The front left-side drum smashes into the stonework. Like brakes have been slammed full on, they're all sent sliding forward on the slippery-wet planks.

Then *THUD!* again. Now they're right under the bridge and in the darkness they can feel the water dragging down one side of the raft, scraping the oil drums hard up against the pillar. Fran's on her feet, shoving and shoving her clothes pole at the stone, hardly able to see what she's doing she tries to push-push-push them free. There's the smell of wet, of water-slime. The current races; its swirl-and-slap, swirl-and-slap sound comes echoing back from the curve of stonework arching above them. Again and again, Steve hauls Nessie back to stop her getting in Fran's way, and to stop her barking.

Then suddenly they're through! Shooting out into the open moonlight again, the current pushing them forward. Moments later they've reached calm water.

For several seconds no one moves, no one speaks. As the current eases, they begin to slow down and then to drift again at their normal speed. Steve can feel his heartbeat steadying as well. Nessie's back to her usual soft-fur self again – except that now she's sitting up alert, ears cocked and looking ahead into the darkness to catch sight of any more bridges, ready to chase them away.

'Did we take on much water?' asks Fran.

'I'm soaked,' Dan replies. 'Water was flying every-where. But that oil drum really smashed into the pillar.'

Steve moves into Mr Optimism mode. 'We didn't hit it *so* hard – and we're still afloat. We can check it later, once we're a bit further from the town.'

Fran's already slid over to check the damage. 'Shh!' She puts her ear to the drum.

They wait. The steady trickle of water beneath them sounds the same as before, comforting almost, and there's that slight, familiar tug every few seconds as the raft settles itself back into the slow and shifting current.

Steve holds his breath as if he's listening, too.

Then Fran turns to them again. 'Fine, no leak in that one.' There's relief in her voice. 'Dan, you do the middle drum, and when he's done, Steve, you take the rear one.'

A quick systems check shows them the drums are all fine. Good as new.

'After a crash like that the raft'll need a re-spray at the garage!' says Dan, which makes them all laugh.

Time for a celebratory Tunnock's caramel wafer each. Nessie does well out of it.

Tunnock eaten, Dan's soon back to being Mr Doom. 'How soon till the next bridge?'

Which makes them think. Out of town you don't really notice bridges. Maybe you get driven across them, or you cycle over them, but you hardly ever notice them. If only he'd brought a map, thinks Steve. He's the oldest so he should have thought of it. But he didn't. He brought Tunnock's wafers instead, as well as his dad's wind-up torch, of course, and some other stuff, but no map. Here they are, going into unknown territory full of dangerous bridges, rapids and maybe even whirlpools and, thanks to him, they've only got caramel wafers to guide them. *Nice one*, he thinks.

'I brought a map,' announces Fran. 'Nicked it out the garage shop, just in case.'

Dan grins. 'You're the best!'

As he watches Fran bending over to unzip a side pocket on her rucksack, it seems to Steve that in some ways she's older than him – which she's not, of course. But somehow she is.

With the map spread open on deck, they kneel round it. Steve brings out his dad's torch, winds it up to full brilliance, then, glancing up every so often to make sure they're keeping well to the middle of the river, they trace their course downstream. He points the beam down low so no one on the bank will see it. He can do that, at least. Seems there's no bridges for miles – none that are marked, anyway.

'I've another two hours on watch,' says Fran. 'Into your sleeping bags, you two.'

Lying there, eyes closed, listening to the reassuring slow trickle of water beneath, Steve remembers he hasn't mentioned meeting Mr Norbett and that the old man might have contacted his parents. What with bringing Nessie, setting off so quickly, then coming to the bridge, it went clean out of his mind. Maybe the whole town's already looking for them? But before he manages to tell them, he's fallen fast asleep.

5

Bright sunlight's shining on Steve when he wakes up. The full-on glare's hitting him right in the face and—

But where's his bedroom gone? His bed? What's he doing out here? Out in the middle of . . .

Then he remembers.

The raft.

Only it's not floating down the river any longer. Seems they've washed up on some shingle, the current nudging them forward every few seconds, but not strong enough to push them further up onto the shore. FranDan are still fast asleep – so much for them keeping watch! Nessie blinks open her eyes and touches the back of his hand with her paw to say good morning.

The sand-and-shingle shore fills a low-lying bend in the river and runs up to a grass bank that's part of a field of cows, some of them leaning over their fence, checking him out. On the other side is a cornfield. Not a house in sight. Dan was supposed to be second watch – and *he's* still in his sleeping bag, so Fran didn't wake him. She must have fallen asleep on her watch. Their leader. This is Steve's chance to show them both – and so, as quietly and slowly as he can, he eases himself out of his sleeping bag. With as little noise as possible he's just stepping down onto the pebbles when –

Scratch! Scrabble! Scrape! Nessie's jumped off the raft to join him, waking up everyone.

'What – what?' Dan jerks bolt upright like he's still half in a dream and half wakening, but doesn't know which half's which.

Fran sticks her paddle over the side. 'So, we've landed then? Where are we?'

Good question.

Steve says he doesn't know. Adds that he was going to gather wood for a fire and brew up some tea before waking everyone.

'Best to unload our stuff first,' suggests Fran, 'then get the raft out of sight.' She glances quickly up and down the river. 'We can paddle it to where that tree's branches are half in the water. Hide it behind them.'

Dan starts passing down their stuff – the rucksacks,

sleeping bags, the food. Fran and Steve carry everything up onto the shingle. Nessie stands guard, keeping a close eye, and an even closer nose, on the food bags.

Fran puts one of them down. 'Should last us a few days, at least. By then we'll have sorted out what we're going to do about—'

Dan's shouting: 'Hey! Hey! Help!'

They turn and . . .

And see the raft floating off out into the river, Dan still on it, waving his arms. 'Help! Help!'

Fran and Steve rush to the water's edge. The raft's already several metres from the shore, heading to midstream and picking up speed every second.

'Help! Help!'

Steve yells, 'Paddle it!'

'No paddle. Help!'

Fran's already splashing out into the river. 'It's not so deep, Dan! Jump off, and you can pull the raft back to—'

Dan jumps. The water's not even halfway up to his waist – he stands and grins at them. 'It's a bit cold!'

Next moment Steve's dashed in as well. Running through water's really hard work when you're wearing

38

jeans and trainers, not at all like swimming. He starts wading as fast as he can.

Fran's almost reached her brother. 'Don't just stand there, Dan. Grab hold of the raft!'

It's about to go spinning off into the current and get carried downstream, further and further from the shore. Dan turns round and makes a grab for it – useless. He's far too late. It's drifted at least three or four metres away from him now, to where the river's flowing much more rapidly.

'We've got to get it back,' cries Fran. 'It might come near the bank close to those trees.' She's dashing back to the shore, Dan following behind. It'd be great fun kicking the water, getting drenched through in their clothes, but there's no time to enjoy it. The three of them rush up onto the shingle then start racing along the bank, shifting into top gear, powering along at full speed. They've got to catch up with the raft, got to grab hold of it. The bend with the overhanging tree is about two hundred metres ahead. Glancing across every few seconds to see if they're going to make it in time, they break every Olympic record in the book as they pound over the grassy bank.

They come to a fence. Hand on the post, big jump and swing over. Nessie's having the time of her life and barking her head off. She hardly stops, sliding belly-down under the bottom strip of barbed wire then streaking on ahead.

Steve's first to reach the bend, the raft thundering towards him. The water's deeper here, no sloping shore, no shingle. A straight drop down from the bank to deep water. Holding onto one of the branches, he leans out as far as he can. He stretches and stretches . . . still no good. Not far enough.

Fran arrives a moment later.

'That branch!' she yells.

He sees it – a long branch growing more or less straight out from the bank and about half a metre above the water. If he's going to grab hold of the raft, he'll need to walk out along it. The river's a lot narrower here, the current much faster. The raft'll be level any second, and he'll only have one chance to get hold of it.

The branch sways a bit as he stands on it; it dips under his weight but feels solid enough. His trainers are slip-and-slithery with the wet.

'Be careful, Steve.'

Too right. Luckily there's another branch straight above to hold onto.

Quickly as he can, he step-slides out along the slippery bark, the branch dipping more and more with every inch. Soon it's touching the surface, and then he takes another step and the water's rushing over his trainers.

The good news is that the raft seems to have got itself snagged in some small branches. Another step-slide and it'll be almost within reach. Gripping tight as he can onto the branch above, he hauls himself closer. The water's now up to his knees, the current trying to drag him deeper.

Another two slide-steps and he'll make a grab for the top of the nearest oil drum.

Like it's coming from a million miles away, he hears Nessie barking with excitement at how this game is just getting better and better. Nearer, he hears Fran urging him to go further and further, like she believes he can do it.

Which he can, and he *will*.

Another half-step, half-slide and the water's well up

his thighs, the swift current tugging at him, tugging hard. He's at full stretch to keep hold of the branch above, he can hardly—

CRACK!

Next instant he's waist-deep in water, and sinking fast, hanging for dear life onto the branch above, dangling in mid-air and mid-water. The branch he was standing on has snapped clean away. It bobs up to the surface and starts to float off.

The raft is already turning in the current, drifting free of the broken branch. One last effort. Maybe if he can . . .

And suddenly the raft has gone.

He wades near enough back to the bank for Fran to take hold of his hand and pull him ashore. Side by side, they stand and watch the raft settling itself in midstream before continuing to float away slowly and steadily downriver and off into the distance.

Once they've made their way back to the shingle beach Fran moves into action. 'Dan!' she calls over her shoulder. 'Get some wood to build a fire – we'll need to get into dry clothes.' She gives Steve a friendly pat on his arm. 'You were great. Did your best. Couldn't be helped. Really great!'

He's dripping wet and starting to chill – he might be freezing to death, even – but he feels the warmth of her smile all over him.

Suddenly, Dan cries out, 'The tent! It's not here! It's still on the raft!'

Steve glances quickly round to check – their sleeping bags, rucksacks, their stores. No tent!

Dan looks stricken: 'What'll we do? What'll we do?'

6

A quarter of an hour later, they've changed into dry clothes and are sitting around a blazing fire sharing a bottle of cola and more biscuits, with a tin of meat for Nessie. No raft any more, and no tent. Nobody wants to just give up and go back home, but what else can they do? Steve says surely they're bound to find an empty shed, an empty barn, an empty something, somewhere. Fran agrees. Dan says nothing.

Steve shrugs. 'Worst case scenario would be us back at school, so let's at least enjoy sitting out here in the sun. Even if it's only for a short time.'

'Worst case scenario would be if we'd drowned when we hit that bridge,' Dan corrects him.

Fran grins. 'Well said, little brother!'

Suddenly there are smiles all round and for a brief moment it feels like they're on the best holiday ever.

Except, where are they? They look round to see if anything's familiar, but it's mostly fields on both sides of the river – cows here, sheep on the opposite bank, a large field of bright yellow rapeseed further downstream, and small woods scattered all over. No houses or roads in sight. The only real landmark is a hill. It's long and lumpy and running vaguely in line with the river, but several miles away.

Dan gives a shout: 'That hill, I've seen it before!' He says he recognises the patches of rock face that show between trees near the top – he's sure it's called after some kind of ice cream. They open up the map, and there it is, Vennel Hill. 'Yeah! Like vanilla.' Seems they're about twenty miles from town.

Feeling warmed by the fire as well as by Fran's smile, Steve begins to feel relaxed.

Too relaxed. For, without thinking what he's doing, he automatically reaches into his pocket for his mobile, to check for messages.

Fran's right on his case. 'You were supposed to leave that at home.'

'I . . . I forgot. Must have slipped it in without—'

'Switch it off, Steve. No Facebook, no Twitter, no—'

'I get it. I get it.'

'We don't want all that stuff. We're here to get away from Thor and his—'

'I get it, Fran. But there's loads of texts from my mum and dad. I said I'd phone them, so that's what I'll do. It's *all* I'll do. No Facebook, no Twitter, Instagram, Snapchat. Nothing. OK?' Without waiting for her reply he dials home.

Before he can get a word in, his mum's shouting at him. 'Where are you? Where are you?'

So he tells them again all about needing some space, too much stress . . .

'We read your note, Steve. Where are you?'

And there's too much pressure at school, he tells them. But he's fine. Fine. They're not to worry. Definitely Not To Worry. He'll be back in a few days.

'Where are you? Where—'

Time to switch to Plan B. 'You're breaking up, Mum . . . Bad connection . . . Can't hear you . . . Can't hear . . . Love you . . .'

He cuts the call.

'Good,' says Fran. 'Now turn it off.'

'Yeah?'

'Completely off. No mobile means no Thor, and gives us time to come up with a plan.'

Silence.

'But what happens when our food runs out?' says Dan.

'There's fish,' Steve replies. 'We can catch fish.'

'Bring a rod, hooks, a net, did you?'

'Rabbits, then. Like I said, Nessie can come with us to catch—'

'Oh yeah?'

At the sound of her name Nessie looks up. She's about to rest her head back down on her paws when she cocks her ears at some crows having an early morning squabble a few trees upstream. The crows caw at each and flap around for a moment before losing interest and dropping back down to the ground. She settles again.

Another silence.

Steve gives her a pat. Yesterday, it had all seemed so simple. Not a word to anyone, just sailing away from all the bullying and badness. Take some time out from Thor and his Vikings, from grown-ups killing off tigers and polar bears, turning ordinary kids and their parents

47

into refugees. Didn't seem much to ask for just a few days away on their own, but now . . .

Suddenly Dan jumps to his feet. 'We don't need a tent! I know somewhere we can go, and be safe. Better than any tent in the world.'

Steve shrugs. 'What difference will it make? Like you say, the food'll run out and—'

Fran puts her fingers to her lips. 'Shh! Someone's coming.'

Voices. Not close, but definitely coming this way.

7

Crouching down low and moving as quietly as they can, they kick out the fire and heap sand and gravel on it. While FranDan gather up their stuff, Steve creeps upriver to the corner where the river bends. Lying with his stomach flat on the ground, he peers through the long grass and sees two men, maybe half a mile upstream, getting themselves ready for a day's fishing. They're far enough away just now, but in time they'll work down towards them. He crawls back to report.

A few moments later the three of them are skirting the field of cattle and doing their best to keep Nessie from rounding them up by feeding her small pieces of caramel wafer every few metres. Dan's in front, having offered to lead them to what he calls 'a safe house like in spy films'.

'Well, it's not a house exactly,' he adds.

All those sorry-looking refugees he saw on TV, thinks Steve, that's just what the three of them must look like now, walking-walking-walking through unknown country, everything on their backs, fleeing the threat of destruction. Except their homes and lives aren't in ruins. If he feels bad – fed up with bullies and school and the constant terrifying news cycle – it's nothing compared to how bad it must feel being a refugee. Sometimes Steve can imagine hacking into the world's mainframe and freezing everything. Freezing time itself. Then he would stop the bombs in mid-air from falling onto innocent kids and their families in Syria, stop politicians in mid-yak-yak-yak with all their excuses, stop the ice caps from melting so polar bears would still have something to stand on, stop little kids younger than him from getting turned into child soldiers, child workers and child slaves, stop bullies like Thor—

'We turn right here, I think,' Dan calls out, then starts going uphill. 'ETA in an hour at most.'

They cross over a road, but it's only a narrow B road and there's no traffic, then through some woods, across a field, another wood, over a footbridge and along the bank of a stream. Every so often Nessie becomes their scout and scampers on ahead to check things out. But they've seen no one apart a farmer sitting high up on his tractor in the middle of an empty field. Maybe he'd be pleased to be 'frozen' – it might stop him feeling lonely out there. Maybe he wouldn't even notice the difference?

The path starts going uphill again, not so steep, not really, not yet, but they can see it's going to get hard soon. It hasn't been used much – tangles of long grass and weeds line what's most likely a sheep track with, every so often, little heaps of black sheep droppings like miniature dried-up ball bearings, and nettles, lots and lots of nettles, and bushes. Soon be the longest day of the year and it's getting warmer and warmer, and Steve's getting hotter and hotter with the weight of his rucksack and having to keep waving away the flies, which just come straight back anyway. Sweat's running down his face.

'This *safe house*, Dan – what kind of place is it?'

'You'll see. It'll be great. Best ever.'

'But you said it's not a house?'

It's not often Dan knows something that other people don't, so he really makes the most of it. 'I'll give you a clue – it's not a *real* house, but someone used to live there.'

'Some kind of shed? A barn? A caravan?' Trying to guess takes Steve's mind off the flies, at least.

'No, not a shed, or a barn, or a caravan. I'll give you another clue – there's no door, no windows, and nobody built it.'

'But someone lived there?'

'Yeah! For years and years.' Dan's loving this – he's grinning, exploding almost from the excitement of knowing something Steve doesn't.

'Ah, yes!' Fran calls out. 'I remember now – Uncle Todd.'

'Don't tell him!'

'Your Uncle Todd stayed there? I thought he lived in a bungalow.'

'He does,' says Fran, 'but he showed us this place one day when we—'

'Let *me* tell it,' interrupts Dan. 'I thought of it. See, Steve, there was this Sunday picnic we *had* to go on, really lame. Longest Sunday on record. We said we wanted to visit a theme park with roller coasters and ice cream, but they said that we didn't know what we wanted because we hadn't seen it yet.'

'I've not seen it either.'

'Are you sure this is the right path, little brother?'

'Yes. I remembered it when I saw we were near the vanilla hill. We're climbing it now and we'll be there before you know it.'

And all at once they are.

The path has been getting steeper and steeper and the flies getting thicker and stickier, when suddenly the track stops going uphill. The ground becomes flat, opening out into a stretch of grass with rocks and boulders scattered everywhere. Some of them must have broken off and fallen down from the crags above. None are falling today though, and haven't for a long while, by the looks of the moss and plants growing in their cracks. There are bushes as well, and more sheep droppings. From nearby there's a splashing sound that must be a waterfall.

'We're here.' Dan's pulling off his rucksack. Fran too.

Steve stares around him. 'Where?'

'Told you you'd be here before you knew it!'

'OK, smart guy, show me.'

'Try and *see* it.' Dan's bursting to tell, and points straight ahead to the steep rock face rising up out of the ground in front of them. 'Look.'

So Steve looks ... and he looks ... and he looks ...

53

A hundred metres of sheer rock. Are they supposed to climb up it or what?

'Perfect, isn't it!'

'Perfect? I don't see anything.'

'That's what's so *perfect*.' Dan's almost hugging himself in glee. 'We'll be safe here.'

Fran starts to walk towards the foot of the crag. 'Come on, Steve, if you come round—'

'I'll show him!' cries Dan. 'I'm going to show him! I thought of it!'

'OK, you show him,' says Fran in her indulgent big-sister voice.

And he does. And he's right. Steve has to admit it really is perfect.

8

'This way.' Dan goes between two tall bushes till he's standing right behind them. Then, abruptly, he disappears. Steve follows him.

It's a cave. A really big cave, as if the rock face has opened its mouth and is keeping it open wide enough for people to walk into.

'Sure it's safe enough to go in?'

'Yeah, come on!' Dan's voice echoes off the cave roof. 'Uncle Todd told us that a hermit used to live here, said he stayed for more than twenty years.'

'Really?'

The floor is bare stone, covered with countless small rock fragments that scrunch underfoot.

'Yeah. He was so fed up with the world and other people that he wanted to live all by himself, and without having to see other people, so he came here. Grew his hair right down to his waist and had a beard like one of these bushes.'

55

Dan tramples over the loose stones, his footsteps echoing all around him. At its highest the roof reaches to about three metres, and the walls go nearly straight up for a metre at the sides before starting to curve inwards to make the ceiling. One corner's been marked off with a line of stones.

'That bit is where he slept. And there's even two parts to the place.' They go through a low gap that leads into a smaller cave. 'This is like the spare bedroom, but with its own entrance. It can be Fran's room.'

When they go back outdoors, Steve sees that the mouth of the smaller cave is as well concealed as the main one, this time behind a massive moss-covered boulder. Dan was right – the caves are completely hidden.

'We'll gather bracken and stuff for sleeping on, and there's a waterfall round the side of the crag that we drank from last time. 'And here ...' Dan leads them over to a shallow hole in the ground ringed by blackened stones. 'This is his fire pit where he did his cooking.' He grins. 'Cool place, eh? A two-room cave complete with running water and all mod cons!'

Upgrading their cave to five-star luxury takes them

less than ten minutes. They gather enough bracken and branches to make mattresses for the bed areas, add some softer ferns for extra comfort, then lay their sleeping bags on top. And that's the three of them moved in! The running water's less than a minute away and tastes deliciously sweet and cold after their hot trek. The perfect en suite!

While Fran arranges their larder of tins and biscuits, Steve gathers more branches and ferns to make a bed for Nessie. Leaving her to explore her luxury bed and sniff her way all round her new home, he goes outside to sit with his back against one of the big boulders, staring out across the valley and beyond. It's the best hideout ever and high enough above the surrounding countryside to see over the woods and fields and all the way down to the river. From here it'll be easy to keep watch and guard against anyone trying to sneak up on them. He looks for any sign of their raft, but it must be long gone.

'Steve, you've got to see this!'

Dan comes running up. 'Got a signal round the side of the crag – my Facebook page – hundreds of posts – we're

really famous – our pictures all over TV, the internet – we've gone viral and – we should write a blog and—'

Fran dashes out of her cave, grabs his phone and switches it off. 'I told you – no phones! They could be used to track our location.' She's back to her mother-knows-best voice. 'Don't you worry, little brother, we'll fix Thor. I'm working on a plan.'

'Hmm.' Steve would like to come up with a plan himself. But clearly there's to be none of that PC, equal-opportunities stuff with Fran. *She's working on a plan.* End of story.

She gives Dan his phone back, but looks about ready to commit murder – she's all dark and intense-looking, despite her blonde hair. Then she grins. 'We'll nail him! Him and his Vikings. In the meantime, keep it switched off. Trust me.' Then she adds, 'Let's make the rest of the day a holiday!'

Their holiday starts well. After a lunch of biscuits, chocolate, coke and a tin of ham – thanks to the tin opener Fran brought – they go for an explore round the hill to get a feel for the area and then venture down the path they'd come up earlier to try guddling for trout in a small stream. Good fun, but not if you're hoping to catch something to eat. Next time they'll use a branch, some string and a bent pin with a worm on it.

It's getting on for teatime as they start back up the track to the cave and they're feeling really good. They've got some tins of food left, the sun's shining and there's still more to come of this perfect summer's day. Every so often, Nessie gallops ahead to go nosing into bushes or racing to the next bend in the path. A flock of birds swoops close and she goes completely mental chasing them. A squirrel shoots out right in front of her – and she's onto it. Nearly. It must be an electric squirrel, the speed it's got, a streak of lightning that shoots up the nearest tree, leaving her at the bottom barking her head off.

'Nessie's hungry,' says Fran.

'Who isn't!' laughs Steve.

Starting a fire to heat up a couple of tins of stew will take ages, but cold stew spooned straight out of a tin tastes like cold sick with dollops of extra lard in it, only worse.

Nessie can't wait even for cold sick and has dashed straight into the caves, tail in the air, nosing about – looking for mice, most likely.

Ten minutes later they've got a fire started, using silver birch bark instead of paper. Steve picks up one of the tins and calls Nessie. She doesn't come. He shouts 'Biscuits!' but still no Nessie. Instead, he hears her up in Fran's cave, frantically scrabbling away at the loose pebbles.

'Biscuits! Biscuits!' he calls as he goes after her. Could've saved his breath – she doesn't even look up from scraping away at a heap of stones piled against the wall. Some of them look really sharp – she'll hurt her paws.

He tries to pull her back, but she's too strong for him. She won't budge, and keeps on scrabbling and scrabbling. Once he's cleared away some of the stones she lunges forward and starts scrabbling even harder. She's gone manic.

He calls to the others outside. 'Dan, Fran – can you come here? I think Nessie's found something.'

Dan yells back, 'Just seeing to the fire. We'll be eating soon.'

'Never mind the fire – come and hold Nessie.'

Fran stands up. 'You do the stew, Dan. I'll see to Nessie.'

Next moment, she's crouching down next to Steve, her arms tight round Nessie's neck, holding her back. 'What is it?'

'I don't know.' He lifts away a large stone and throws it – *CRASH!* – to one side.

He throws aside more stones – *CRASH! CRASH! CRASH!*

'Bring the torch, Dan,' shouts Fran.

Nessie's more and more frantic.

Next moment, Dan's standing above them, shining the torch down. 'Maybe it's a body? Maybe someone was buried here where no one would ever—'

'Too small for a body.' With his sleeve Steve wipes aside the last of the small stones and pebbles to reveal a flat piece of rock like a roof slate. He sees now that the heap of loose stones had been placed on top just for show – the better to conceal what's hidden underneath.

Steve's about to reach inside the hidey-hole when he feels Fran pulling him back.

'Careful, Steve. You don't know what's in there. Take it slow.'

True enough. He pauses.

'Yeah,' adds Dan. 'Might be booby-trapped – a trip wire or something set to blow the place apart the moment somebody touches it and then we'd all be—'

'Thank you, Dan. I get the idea. But this far from everywhere, and stuffed in here out of sight, I don't think that—'

Before anyone can stop her, Nessie's lunged forward and stuck both paws under the flat stone and begun scrabbling furiously.

'Run!' shouts Dan, but nobody moves.

Scrabble-scrabble-scrabble. They wait.

No explosion.

Steve hauls Nessie out of the way and reaches into the hole. His fingers grab hold of something. Not hard like stone, not soft either. He takes a firm grip and slides it out.

9

It's a large bag, canvas, quite heavy and covered in rock dust. Not one of those shopping-sized bags for tourists, but bigger, more like a sack.

'There's writing on it. Bring the torch closer, Dan.'

He wipes away some of the dust. The bag's green. 'Army Property. Authorised Personnel Only.' It's zipped tight shut.

It's a soldier's kitbag. 'What would anyone want to hide a—'

Having broken free from Fran, Nessie once again starts pawing frantically at it.

'Maybe it's hidden treasure!' cries Dan.

Fran rubs her hand along the canvas. 'Think it's been there long?'

Steve shrugs, then moves into CSI mode. 'Difficult to tell. No sign of wearing, no mould or scratch marks that would indicate animal activity.'

'Except for Nessie.'

The bag's a magnet to her; they no sooner haul her out of the way than she shoves herself back on top of it, sniffing, scraping, pawing.

'Hope it's not body parts,' says Dan

'A body would've been dumped somewhere out in the woods,' says Steve, still in CSI mode, 'buried deep so it would rot back into the earth and disappear for good. The perfect crime. We'll take it outside to see better.'

They settle down in the sun, the kitbag in front of them.

'Suppose someone comes back for it?' says Dan. 'They could, at any time. Today, even.'

'Not really. Might've been there for years.'

'Ex-army? Might be some seriously heavy-duty dudes from Special Ops, or the SAS. We should leave it alone. Then, when they do come, we can say we don't know—'

'What? Hi there, dude, and by the way we don't know anything about your kitbag?'

'No. I mean—'

'It's too late now,' points out Fran. 'Best see what's inside anyway, then we'll work out what to do.'

She looks at Steve. Steve nods back.

They shake it. Things shift about inside. The zip seems rusted stuck.

Dan's on his feet. 'Might be gold bars.'

There's a moment's silence as they think about gold bars, like they've seen in films.

'Must belong to somebody,' he adds.

'Ours now,' says Fran.

They think about being rich. Really, really rich. Gold bar rich.

'But Nessie wouldn't be so excited about gold bars,' says Steve. 'Maybe she's a natural sniffer dog and it's drugs.'

Drugs, they know, would be bad news. Drugs would mean thugs, drugs would mean violence and people getting hurt. Them most likely.

Steve lifts up the bag. 'You two hold it straight and I'll try the zip. It feels pretty stiff.'

'If it is gold bars we'll all be at Disneyland this time next week, staying in a five-star hotel!' Dan looks hopeful.

'And keep Nessie out the way, I nearly unzipped her nose!'

One final tug and the zip slides open.

'That's it.' Steve's about to put in his hand . . .

'Don't,' says Fran, stopping him. 'Might be anything inside there. Best to lay it flat on the ground and slide—'

But before the others can stop him, Dan's grabbed the bag and is shaking it out, emptying everything onto the grass.

At once, Nessie's right in there, leaping in front of them and getting totally in the road – head and paws everywhere. They have to drag her away.

No gold bars. No drugs either.

Lots of familiar-looking packets, though, dozens of them.

'What on earth would anyone want to . . . ?'

'Useful at least.' Fran reads out a few of the labels. 'Minestrone, chicken and veg, mushroom . . .'

There are packets of dried soup, dried veg, noodles and even more packets of dried meat. No wonder Nessie was frantic. The meat's vacuum-packed, the kind that doesn't need to be kept in a fridge. Also some pasta, rice, tinned sardines, tinned tuna, chocolate and energy bars.

'No Disneyland for us,' Fran laughs, 'but at least we'll eat well from now on.'

'Wait, there's more.'

As well as a roll of black duct tape there are two parcels like bricks wrapped in thick plastic, taped to keep them firmly sealed and waterproof.

Dan edges away. 'That'll be drugs, I'm telling you. We've got to leave. Take some of the food and put everything else back.'

Fran and Steve look at each other. Again there's no need to speak.

Steve takes out his Swiss Army knife – best birthday present ever – to start on the smaller parcel. It's brick-shaped but much lighter. He slices through the tape. It's a heavy-duty plastic bag that's been carefully folded over and over to make it tight and compact.

'Don't put your hand straight inside, Steve. Best to ease it out slowly. Whatever *it* is.'

He nods at her. There's total silence as he lifts the bag up by the bottom to let the contents gradually slide out.

Then, at the last moment, he whips it free like a magic trick. 'Hey presto!'

For a moment, they all stare down at what's dropped onto the ground.

'My God!' says Fran. She's speaking for all of them. 'Look at that!'

They're gobsmacked. Utterly.

10

Lying on the grass in front of them is a thick wad of banknotes. The one at the top's a fifty. None of them have ever seen a fifty before. It's red.

'Must be thousands!' says Fran.

'Thousands and thousands!' says Steve.

'Thousands and thousands and thousands!' says Dan.

They stare at it. Take turns at holding the bundle, removing the elastic band and riffling through the notes like they're a pack of cards, trying to guess how many, and how much. It's fifties all the way through.

Fran starts to count them and gives up after £3000. 'Must be £30,000 at least.'

Then Dan says what they're probably all thinking, but wish they weren't. 'Heavy-duty dudes, like I said. Seriously heavy duty. This is their gang money. Their secret stash. Has to be.'

They put the wad back on the ground again where, with the silver strip on the top note catching the bright sunlight, it glitters back at them. Thirty thousand plus seems to have an energy all of its own.

They turn to the other packet.

'This one *must* be drugs. I'm telling you,' says Dan. 'We should leave it. Just leave it and go. They could come for it at any moment. They'll be the sort of guys that hang out at the Wild West but worse, much worse. While we still have the chance we should—'

Steve holds up his hand for silence. Again Fran and he look at each other. Again nothing needs said.

The other pack's only slightly bigger, but twice as heavy. Steve takes it in both hands. Then, like one of those TV pathology cops, he pick up his knife and starts slicing the tape. Another bag – he empties it out onto the ground.

'Oh my God!' they all cry out, this time in chorus.

Dan jumps to his feet. 'I'm out of here.' And before the others can stop him, he's run back into the cave where he rushes about like a headless chicken – a demented headless chicken. He's panic-shouting: 'We gotta go! We gotta go!'

Fran and Steve ignore him. Because they're staring, fascinated. Shocked.

11

Neither of them has seen a gun before. Not a real one, not like this. Only in films. Steve's handled air rifles, of course, and one time was even given the local gamekeeper's shotgun to hold. But airguns and shotguns are for shooting at targets, for shooting crows or rabbits. This is a real gun, a pistol. For shooting at *people*.

It's silver, with a square-ish handgrip where the bullets are kept. In the films the cops always pull back a kind of spring-loaded magazine inside to check the gun's ready for action. Ready to be pointed, aimed and fired – at a real person. To kill.

The noise of Dan clattering about in the cave seems to be coming from miles away, the cave itself seems miles away, as do the bushes, the rocks and giant boulders scattered all around them, the stone crags. The whole world seems to have faded to nothing, leaving only the two of them ... and a real gun lying inches away on the grass.

71

Without thinking what he's doing, Steve reaches forward. His fingers touch the barrel. Solid metal, smooth. Deadly.

Fran's voice is almost a whisper. 'Maybe Dan's right? This is dangerous. Too dangerous.'

His fingers slide up and down the barrel. 'Do you think it's loaded?'

'Wanting to fire it and see, are you? Like it's a new toy?'

She pushes aside some stray hair that's fallen across her face. She's staring right at him, staring hard. 'That what you want to do? Make a big bang that'll tell everyone for miles around that we're here, tell them we've found their gun?'

Truth is – Steve doesn't know what he wants to do. Put it back in the bag and the bag back in its hidey-hole under the stones? Or maybe fire it first? Just the once. Or else join the headless chicken club – throw the gun into the bushes and get the hell away from here as far and as fast as he can?

With his fingers closing around the handle, the gun's a snug fit.

'Careful,' she whispers. 'Just in case . . . it might . . .'

There are slight grooves in the handle he'd not noticed before, and it feels very comfortable to hold, balances well in his hand.

Fran presses her finger on the barrel to make sure it's pointing down at the ground. Her hand remains there for several seconds. Steadying it.

'Do you want to hold it?' asks Steve.

She nods.

He passes it over.

All at once he realises he's angry. Really, really angry. Not with Fran though, but with grown-ups. Bloody grown-ups! He thought they'd got away from them, away from their stupidity, away from their greed and how they're always wanting to hurt people – and yet here they are again! Their money. Their gun.

The three of them could've had some quality time catching fish, making fires, chilling out for a few days. But not any more.

Fran's lifted the gun up and is holding it so she can look along the barrel. He wants to snatch it from her, take it and run all the way down to the river then throw it as far out into the water as he can.

But he knows he won't.

'Probably not loaded,' she says.

Dan rushes up, rucksack in his hand. 'I'll leave you the food, all of it. I'm going home.'

Fran gets to her feet and blocks his path. 'You're going nowhere, little brother. We need to sit down and talk this through. Come to some decision. The three of us, together.'

'No! These guys could turn up at any moment. And when they find out we've—'

Steve stands up. 'Might have been left here ages ago. An emergency stash in case they ever need to hide out. Lie low from the cops, that sort of thing. No reason they'll come today, or tomorrow, this week, this year even—'

'All that money? They'll be back all right, I'm telling you, and then they'll—'

Fran takes the rucksack from him. 'Dan. Sit. Down. When. You're. Told.' There's a real adult-in-charge tone to her voice that Steve's never heard before. He's impressed.

Dan sits down.

Realising she's still holding the gun, Fran lays it on the grass. Very, very carefully.

The three of them stare at it again. It has to be *someone's* gun. A gangster, maybe even a killer. Someone who could – whatever they'd like to think – really *could* appear at any moment to reclaim it. No one speaks.

Suddenly Fran reaches across for one of the meat packets. 'This is long-life stuff – if it's well past its sell-by date, then maybe there's no problem.' She inspects it closely. 'It's best before the twenty-fifth of June this year.'

Which is next week. Not so good. Definitely not so good.

'OK. But it doesn't seem so very urgent that they'll turn up today.' Steve tries to sound upbeat.

He's fooling no one.

Next thing, Dan's got to his feet and started waving the gun around. 'We could go and do Thor now! Bang! Bang! Bang!'

Is he joking?

Without saying a word Fran holds out her hand and Dan gives her the gun. 'I'll put this somewhere safe,' she says. She gets to her feet and goes towards her cave.

Meanwhile, hoping to take Dan's mind off things, Steve tries to open one of the packets. Not so easy. It says 'Peel here' – well, he's peeling and nothing's happening. 'Let's give Nessie a taste,' he says. 'We've got loads. It's salami. A dog's sense of smell is millions and millions of times stronger than ours, did you know that? The smell's driving her berserk. We can—'

Dan's response is a real downer. Typical. 'Maybe it's poisoned. Like it's there to guard the money and the gun. So that anyone who finds them who's not supposed to . . . dies.'

'For goodness' sake, Dan. That's paranoid.'

'Here's us expecting heavy-duty thugs to come and gun us down at any moment, and you say I'm paranoid!

'About the meat, yes.'

'OK, Steve, if you're so sure – then eat some.'

'All right, I will. When I manage to get the packet open, that is.'

Bad timing. Just then the plastic peels back. There's a strong blast of garlic. Nessie almost does a mid-air somersault to grab it.

'You could test it on her first,' suggests Dan. 'That's

what oligarchs and gangster bosses do. I read it online. They feed a few spoonfuls to a low-grade minion to see if he drops dead. Same with Roman emperors.'

Steve looks at Nessie. Her bright eyes. Her eagerness. Her friendly grin. Her total trust. No. He couldn't. He can't. He won't. He pulls off a few slices. It smells delicious. Poison? Not a hint of any poison smell – just sticky, greasy, garlicky salami. But still he hesitates.

He pictures Fran coming back to find him lying stretched out on the ground, looking pale and hardly breathing. Looking *poisoned*. She'll rush up, take his head in her arms. She's in tears. She's sighing and saying his name over and over again. She leans closer. She's about to—

'Come on then, Steve, eat it if you're going to.'

'Right then.' He pops a slice into his mouth. Tastes good. Tastes *very* good. He waits for a second, then starts chewing really fast.

12

Dan's peering closely at him, looking for any signs that he's dying or about to drop dead, or at least going deadly pale or bright red, green or whatever.

Should he pretend? Give the worrywart a real fright?

Why bother? Sometimes Dan's just a dickhead.

He smacks his lips and gives a big swallow. 'Delicious!'

Mr Doom speaks up again. 'Might be a slow poison.'

'Don't give up, do you?' He helps himself to more salami without dropping dead, then holds out the packet. 'Fancy some Death?'

But, instead, Nessie jumps up, her jaws wide open, and snatches it out of his hand. She races off.

Suddenly Fran's returned. 'You shouldn't have let her eat it, Steve. Did you smell it first? Might've been poisoned.'

'Told you!' says Dan.

'Too late now! I've had half a packet already. Really delicious, by the way. You should try some, Fran.'

So much for her cradling him in her arms and weeping over him.

It's what grown-ups always call 'a beautiful evening'. Which means dead calm – dead, like with absolutely *nothing* happening. They're sitting outside the caves; the fire's burned down so it's mostly grey ash with scratch marks of red embers glowing from the last of the wood. They've just eaten their best meal since leaving town. Menu: A choice of cup-a-soup, a whole packet of meat and a tin of spaghetti each. Then chocolate, a whole bar per person. And there's hardly a dent in their new food hoard. Now they're sitting stuffed and staring out at a grown-up's beautiful evening. So stuffed that for once the dead-calm-with-absolutely-nothing-happening feels perfect.

Till out of nowhere, Fran says, 'Here's what we'll do.'

Staying slumped full of dinner and doing nothing is all the boys have got planned for the next few hours, but they manage a nod of interest. Which, thinks Steve, is more than his dad does when he falls asleep in front of the TV. He doesn't want to turn into his dad – so he gives another nod to show some more interest.

Fran carries on: 'We'll wrap up the gun and the money like they were before. We'll put back most of the food, which'll still leave us plenty to last for a few days. Stick the money and the gun on top like it would have been – it was *under* the food when we emptied it out, remember.' She pauses, then carries on, 'Then we put the bag back where it was and cover it over again with rocks and pebbles like before. No one'll know we found it.'

Nod number three. Putting the gun back gets Steve's vote. But putting back the money? All of it?

Fran's still talking. 'Then, just before we leave – in a couple of days, max – we take the money. Otherwise it might just go to waste. Whoever put it there might have left the country, been sent to jail, fallen ill – died, even. Who knows? Maybe no one's ever coming back for it.'

Suddenly Dan's heavy-duty dudes don't seem such a threat any more. It takes about a quarter of an hour to repackage everything as it was and then to slide the bag back into its hidey-hole with some rocks and pebbles heaped on top. Looks the same as when they found it. Exactly the same. They can relax.

It's late now. Everyone's tired.

The boys snuggle down into their sleeping bags. Beneath them, the bracken and twigs crackle every time they shift about or roll over. They call goodnight through to Fran and she calls goodnight back – they shout goodnight to each other back and forth a few times to hear the good-night-night-night-night-night echoing off the walls as if the caves are saying goodnight to them, too.

When Steve lies on his back he can see the entrance framed in the moonlight a few feet away. There's the never-stopping splash of the small waterfall; every few minutes a night bird calls or an owl hoots; sheep make restless noises from somewhere nearby. It's so still and quiet that he can hear everything.

Dan falls asleep almost at once. Steve pictures Fran in her cave next door, listening to the very same sounds as him – the same splashing waterfall, the owls, the sheep. For a last moment, just before he drifts off, he imagines the two of them are the only people in the world and sharing these same sounds together ...

Morning. Low clouds and a wet, bruised-looking sky. It's going to rain later. They share a breakfast of leftover meat, biscuits and chocolate. For afters, Dan clears his throat, looks embarrassed and admits he's just been on Facebook. He reads out Thor's latest post:

So scared that you ran away, did you? The place is much better without you. Let's keep it like that. Don't come back. No one wants you. Get dressed up in your Lidl best and the two of you can hold hands then step in front of a car or even better jump off a cliff. Your choice. Don't try sneaking back. Remember, we know where you live.

'What did he say all that for? And to *us*?'

'I told you not to ... Oh, what's the point?' Fran shakes her head. 'Listen, Dan, Thor's a nobody and needs to give himself a big name to feel big. Bullies like him act like they're still in primary one because they've not grown up. That's *his* problem – and it's not going to be yours. We'll fix him.'

'But he knows where I live!'

'Everybody in town knows where you live,' Steve points out. 'He's bound to be someone in our class, same with his Vikings. He's too scared to use his own name

– that way we'd know him for the joke he is, and just laugh at him.'

'We'll go back in a day or so, little brother, once I've fine-tuned my plan. Then we'll nail him.'

'You've got a plan?'

'Don't worry, it's coming along nicely.'

Fran's glad the boys have gone off fishing. Gives her some peace to think how best to sort out Thor. Her plan's coming along nicely? If only. But she had to say something to Dan, or he'd just worry and worry. Far in the distance, she can see the farmer they saw yesterday on their way here – he's on his tractor again and driving at less than one mile an hour up and down his lonely field. Is that what life's like when you get older? Up and down the same boring field every day – house, kids, job, house, kids, job, over and over.

Having some peace and time to herself is good. She'd been getting bored with the endless boy-noise, boy-mess, boy-clamour for attention.

Whatever. The place needs a tidy up – all those empty food packets and scraped-out tins lying around

everywhere like it's the town dump. Meanwhile she can think about her plan.

Two hours, some clearing up and several rejected Thor plans later, Fran hears Nessie's bark coming from down the path. She jumps to her feet and looks over to the gap in the trees where the boys should be appearing at any moment. Them and their fish – here's hoping! Pity really, another boy-free hour would've been—

BARK! BARK! BARK! Nessie's really going for it. Maybe she's herding them home faster so she can get to the salami sooner. Or the salmon they've caught, who knows?

But wasn't that a growl? That rasping deep-in-her-throat roar like she's—

Furious barking now. And voices. Men's voices. Shouting, yelling, someone swearing at Nessie to shut up.

BARK! BARK! GROWL! GROWL!

Something's wrong. Something's very wrong. Fran jumps to her feet. She needs to get herself out of sight. And quick.

Next moment, she's crouching down in the mouth of her cave, peering round the side of the big boulder.

13

Nessie appears first, running ahead as always. Then she stops and turns around.

BARK! BARK!

She rushes back into the woods again.

BARK! BARK!

Then Dan shoots forward, half-stumbling into the open clearing. He falls over.

BARK! BARK!

Fran's about to rush out and go to help him when—

A man appears. Shaved head. Breeze-block body. Carrying a heavy stick. Like a biker in his denim jacket with cut-off sleeves, jeans, boots. He prods Dan to make him get back on his feet. Steve comes next, being pushed along by another man, red-haired, thin as a bean pole and with another heavy stick. Fran watches as Steve nearly loses his balance as well.

Shavehead's really shouting at them. 'So you moved into our cave, did you? A couple of squatters!'

85

'No, no. Sorry. Really nice place you've …' She can hear the shakiness, the fear, in Dan's voice.

Steve's joined in: 'We've been camping. Found the cave this morning and … didn't know you had … sorry, sorry … get our stuff and go.'

'You wish. Coming to our cave when you're not asked. We don't want visitors. Don't like visitors.' Shavehead spits on the ground. 'You don't get to walk away that easy.'

They're getting nearer, the boys prodded forward at every step. Nessie's circling round and round them, keeping out of range of their sticks, barking like mad.

Fran crouches down even lower.

They're near the fire pit where she'd been sitting only a moment ago.

'We were just fishing, I'm telling you,' explains Steve. 'Then we were going to—'

'Skiving off school, are you?'

Then Red Hair speaks up. 'Hang on, wasn't there something on the TV about a bunch of local kids?'

Dan blurts out, 'Different school, different kids. Only the two of us. There were *three* of them and—'

'Anyway,' adds Steve, 'there's no problem – we're here

86

doing a special project on camping and living rough. See what we've caught – real trout, three of them!'

'Bloody minnows they are! Should've thrown them back!' Shavehead knocks the small fish out of Steve's hand onto the ground, then laughs. It's a jagged, cruel-sounding laugh. 'A long slog up here. We'll get our breath back.' He sits down. There's the familiar *skoosh!* sound of a beer can being opened. 'Then we'll check to see you lads haven't been nosing around where you're not wanted.'

Fran backs away into the cave mouth. She's never been so scared.

Shavehead and Red Hair. Breeze-block and bean-pole. Nasty, the pair of them. Dangerous. Shavehead's arms are blue-scored with tattoos. Must be *their* kitbag.

But what about her sleeping bag and stuff? If the men find it they'll know the boys have been lying. She can't let them find her.

Come on, she psyches herself up. She knows what she has to do. *Come on*. Stepping as quietly as she can on the loose stones, she goes tiptoeing right into the cave. Tiptoeing, but fast. With luck, she might still have a few minutes to do what needs done, but she's got to be quick.

The men continue sipping their beer. The boys have been made to sit between them, with Nessie crouched between *them*, growling every few moments. Steve keeps stroking her to help her stay calm.

'Fancy some?' asks Red Hair.

'No thanks,' says Steve. 'Don't really like it.'

'Poncey wee shit, aren't you?' The biker spits on the ground. He's the scarier of the two, definitely.

The biker's first greeting – 'Hi, lads, how's the fishing?' – as they'd met on the path had sounded wrong to Steve. From the start he knew the men were bad, just *knew* it. Then, as they'd started walking along together, Dan had gone and opened his mouth to tell them about how they were camping up at the caves. Too much information. The usual Dan. That's when the men had turned nasty. Next thing, they'd picked up a couple of broken branches, thick as fence posts, and he and Dan were being prodded and pushed forward at every step, with the biker aiming occasional kicks at Nessie, swiping at her with his stick. And now this threatening silence and not a clue about what's going to happen next – except that he knows it's not going to be good.

Steve's thinking about Fran. She must have got fed up waiting for them to come back from fishing and gone for a walk. But what if she suddenly shows up? Thanks to Dan babbling on like a burst tap, telling them it was just the two of them here – too much information, again – the men would know they'd been lied to. And they wouldn't be pleased. Not these two. No way.

Finally the biker gets to his feet, scrunches up his can and throws it into the bushes. 'While Elvis here stays to keep you company, me and your pal'll check to see you've not been nosing around. Haven't broken anything.'

'Done nothing, broke nothing,' protests Dan.

'Shut it, you. Come on.' Shavehead grabs Dan by the arm, hauls him to his feet and shoves him towards the cave. 'Get moving.'

Steve keeps a tight grip on Nessie's collar. If he lets her go, she might rush up to the cave, annoy Shavehead and end up getting hurt. Red Hair Elvis sits saying nothing, not even glancing at him. Like he knows there's no need because they're just kids, kids he and Shavehead can stomp on any time they want to.

Steve can hear Dan talking the biker through what they've got in the cave. There's a real fear-quaver in his voice. 'That's our food store, mister, just some tins and stuff.'

Don't let Mr Too-much-information say anything about salami or rice, or the man'll suspect they found his kitbag. Fran must have tidied away all the empty food packets, which is really lucky. But where is she? She could show up at any moment and then . . .

But worse – what about her sleeping bag and stuff all over her cave? If the men see that, then they're toast, big time.

'What sort of dog is she?' Elvis is speaking to him. Is that what he's really called? Or is it a joke, his street name maybe? Elvis was some famous singer from ages ago.

'Bit of a mix – border collie, retriever and then some. Nessie's friendly though. Best dog ever.'

'Not that friendly. Growls a lot. What's she eat?'

'Sala— sausages, I mean. She loves sausages.' He'd

nearly said salami. His heart's thumping. 'Really loves them.'

'We had sniffer dogs in Afghanistan. Tough dogs they were. Saved lives, too. Deserve medals, the lot of them.'

'You've been to Afghanistan?'

'Yeah, in the army, both of us. Kojak saved my life once in Helmand when we were out on patrol. When I left the army after my last tour I ended up on the streets – no job, no money, no place to stay – and he saved me again. Bumps into me one day and, well, now I'm fixed up, helping him run his business.'

'Kojak? Is that his real name?' He can see the man's not trying to catch him out, just making conversation. A heavy-duty dude, and yet a bit like Mr Norbett. Only a very, very little bit like Mr Norbett though, and the rest of him is all bad. Some adults are like that – one day they're interested in you, and the next they don't care. Which is the real them and which is them just pretending? Do they even know themselves?

'It's what they called him in the army, cos of his shaved head. Like the cop in the old TV series.'

'CSI?'

'Probably before your time. See my parents, they called me Elvis. Thought a famous name'd give me a good start in life. Well, they got that wrong! Bloody Elvis!'

Steve says it's a cool name – which he knows it isn't, it's really lame – but the man doesn't notice. And Dan? There's not a sound coming from the cave. What's happening with Dan?

'Your dog's called Nessie, yeah?'

He nods.

'What's Nessie eat around here? Not many butchers or pet shops.'

'She catches stuff – does her best anyway. Rabbits, squirrels . . . Me and Nessie, we look after each other.'

Just then Dan appears, clutching both their rucksacks. 'I've packed everything. Man says we're to leave now.'

Thank God. They mustn't have gone into Fran's cave. But what about her stuff? And what about Fran? He and Dan'll have to find her ASAP and make sure she doesn't come back here.

He gets to his feet immediately. 'Goodbye . . . Elvis.'

'Nice meeting you, kid,' says Elvis.

Rucksacks on their backs, they're hurrying across the clearing at double speed.

'Where's Fran gone?' Steve hisses under his breath.

'I don't know,' Dan hisses back. 'She's just ... gone.'

'What about her sleeping bag and everything?'

The two of them have almost reached the edge of the clearing. A few more steps and they'll be safe among the trees.

'We didn't actually go into her cave. The guy took a quick glance in while I was getting our gear packed, probably to check the stones were still piled up on top of his kitbag. Mustn't have even noticed her stuff.'

'But he will, he's bound to. Once we're out of sight, he'll go in there and find it.'

'We've got to get hold of her or else she's—'

The two of them and Nessie are about to head down the path into the wood when Nessie turns and runs all the way back.

As Steve turns to call her, he sees Kojak coming out of Fran's cave, carrying the kitbag. Nessie rushes straight up to him, tail wagging, sniffing and whining with pleasure.

15

'Nessie, come here! Come here!' The boys yell at her, scream at her, but she ignores them. Still calling for her to come, they go a few steps further into the wood, hoping she'll follow.

Some hope.

'Nessie! NESSIE!' Steve returns to the edge of the clearing and bellows at the very top of his voice. 'COME HERE, NESSIE! COME HERE! BISCUITS! BISCUITS!'

But she's gone deaf. Whining, sniffing, tail going like a windmill, paws scrabbling to get inside the kitbag. Food-frantic! Meat-manic!

Steve rushes full speed across the clearing. 'Sorry, Mister Kojak. I'll take her away. A real nuisance. Sees someone with a bag . . . always hoping for food. It's all she thinks about.' He grabs Nessie by the scruff of her neck. Starts pull-pull-pulling her with all his strength. She's hardly budging.

94

Kojak's looks at them, his finger flicking the zip back and forward.

Steve pull-pull-pulls her even harder. Both arms round her neck now, like it's a hundred Nessies he's trying to haul away. 'Come on, Nessie! Come on!' They must must MUST get away! Maybe the men won't notice there's packets of food missing, but they can see that Nessie already knows it's there. Plus, the biker couldn't have missed Fran's stuff when he went in the cave, her spread-out sleeping bag and—

'Get that dog out of here before I—'

'Don't shoot her, please don't.'

But he's said too much. Kojak turns to face him.

'Shoot her? Think I carry a gun, do you?' He looks Steve right in the eye. 'Or maybe I've got one here in my bag?'

'I – I – You've been in the army so I thought ...' His voice has gone very weak.

'Hear that, Elvis? Sonny-boy seems to think I've got a gun in here. Let's see if he's been poking his nose where he shouldn't – and needs taught a lesson.' He grabs the zipper, tugs it open.

'I don't need a lesson. Don't need anything. Come on, Nessie!' Another massive pull. 'Come on, Nessie! See, mister, we're leaving.'

'No, you're not.' Kojak nods to Elvis who grabs Steve by the shoulder.

'Ahhh!' The sudden pain makes Steve cry out.

He's told to sit down. Not to move. Not an inch. The man's fingers dig in deeper. 'Tell your pal to come over here.'

Still keeping a tight grip on Nessie, Steve shouts across. 'Dan! Wait up. Can you come here a minute?'

'Maybe your dog opened the bag all by himself?' sneers Kojak.

Dan's standing next to him now. 'Let us go, please. We won't tell. Nothing to tell. Never saw your bag, never opened—'

Just then Nessie breaks free from Steve's arms, and starts barking and barking.

'SHUT THAT DOG UP, WILL YOU!' Then the man's anger suddenly goes all quiet and cold – the worst kind. 'Let me tell you, sonny-boy, if there is a gun in here, that dog's going to be the first to know.'

'No! No! You wouldn't shoot Ness—'

'Try me.'

Kojak goes a few metres away and empties the bag out on the grass.

'You can shoot me instead,' says Steve.

The biker looks up. 'Are you serious? It's just a dog.'

'No! No! NO! She's Nessie! She's NESSIE!'

'You want it, I'll shoot you as well.' He's throwing aside the packets of food, swearing. Getting furious. 'Can't see it. Can't see it.' He picks up the pack of money. 'Cash is here, right enough, but where the hell's . . .?'

He shakes out the bag again. Empty. He hurls it away, then turns to glare at the two boys. 'You thieving little bastards!'

16

Steve's bewildered. They put everything back in the kitbag. The food, the money, the gun. Everything.

Kojak slaps him across the face, really hard. Then slaps him again, with the back of his hand.

'What've you done with it?'

Steve tries to make his voice sound normal, but can't. 'Done with what? I don't understand—'

Another double slap makes his teeth rattle, his eyes water. There's the taste of blood in his mouth.

'Understand now? You know damn well what I'm talking about. My shooter. You little ...' Kojak looks ready to hit him again, this time with his fist. But at the last minute, he drops his arm and, instead, smiles at him, a smile that's all nails and broken glass, then he picks up one of the meat packets. He rips it open and holds out a handful of salami towards Nessie. 'Here, doggie. It's your lucky day.'

So far Nessie's been looking on, barking and whining

and getting really distressed. But not any more. She might not understand what's been happening to Steve and Dan, but she understands food, especially salami, and so she rushes up and snaps at it. Hardly a chew, just one gulp and it's gone. At once, she's all eagerness for more.

Kojak holds out another slice, letting her come really close while keeping the slice gripped tight between his fingers so she's forced to gobble it down a tiny bit at a time.

He grabs hold of her. 'Got you!' He locks his arm round her neck.

He feeds her another slice, then he takes a knife out of his denim jacket. 'Called *Nessie*, yeah? A good way to go, no? While she's enjoying herself?' He looks over her head at Steve. 'Now, sonny-boy – WHAT . . . HAVE . . . YOU . . . DONE . . . WITH . . . MY . . . SHOOTER?'

'Nothing, nothing. I've not done nothing with nothing, mister. You've got to believe me. Honest. Honest.'

Cold, cold anger now. 'Then again I might not kill her. Not immediately.' He holds the knife up to the side of Nessie's face. 'Got such soft eyes, hasn't she?'

 99

Before Steve can speak, Dan blurts out, 'We put everything back in your bag, we did. Everything. Your gun as well.'

'You've both been little liars, haven't you?'

'We were scared, mister,' says Steve. 'That was all. Finding a real gun – it spooked us. We put everything back. You've got to believe us. Put it all back. Everything. We really, really did.'

'You lied last time.' He strokes the top of Nessie's head with the blade of his knife. 'Likely you're lying now. Once a liar, always a liar. That's right, isn't it, Elvis?'

The other man nods. 'Always.'

'Elvis – their rucksacks.'

The red-haired man pulls off Steve's backpack, opens it and empties it out on the ground. Using his foot he kicks aside the sleeping bag, the spare T-shirt, socks and underwear, his toilet bag, his dad's torch. 'Nothing there.'

He does the same with Dan's. Again nothing.

'You've got to believe us,' pleads Steve. 'We're telling you the truth. We wrapped up the money and the gun just like we found them, and stuck the bag under the pile of stones so no one would notice. We knew it had to be really bad men who—'

'You got that right, sonny. We're really bad men, bad as they come. Your worst nightmare.'

17

Then, to Steve's surprise, Kojak lets Nessie go. But, of course, she doesn't go far. She remains a few feet away, hoping for more salami.

'Remember, sonny-boy, I only need to hold out a piece of meat and she'll come running to me.'

True enough. She'd follow anyone for the chance of food. Nessie's all stomach and no sense.

'One step out of line from either of you, one word we don't like the sound of, and . . .' Kojak stabs at the air with his knife and then pretends to wipe the blade on the side of his jeans. 'Do you believe them, Elvis?'

'Does believing them even matter?'

'If I knew where it was, I'd tell you,' says Steve. Too right he would. He'd give the man his gun gift-wrapped in all the plastic and duct tape he could ever want.

A moment later, they're pushed into Fran's cave. Steve's made to show them the hidey-hole under the heap of stones. 'That's where we found your bag and put it back after. With everything in it — just like it was.'

Suddenly he notices that Fran's stuff isn't there. It's completely vanished. Her sleeping bag, rucksack — like she'd never even been near the place. Magic? Or did she just take off the moment they'd left to go fishing? Had enough of him and Dan, packed up and headed home?

Kojak kicks at the loose stones, making a loud clatter of echoes.

'Right then, outside!'

Back outdoors, the two men start arguing in low voices — it seems that Kojak's saying they should do something and Elvis is saying no, they shouldn't, they should do something else. It's not clear what they're arguing about, but every so often one or other of them glances over to where Steve and Dan are standing, getting more frightened by the moment. They're too terrified to speak, to move even. When Nessie comes up to them, wagging and grinning and friendly as ever — always pleased-to-see-them Nessie, Nessie who hasn't a clue about what's going on — they hardly even glance at her.

Argument over, Kojak turns round to them and points to a nearby boulder that's low and flat. 'Empty out your pockets.'

They do so, laying the things out on the rock. Some coins, homemade fish hooks, a couple of energy bars, a piece of string, their mobiles.

'You won't be needing these any more.' He hurls Steve's mobile against the boulder, smashing it to bits. 'Time for an upgrade, eh?' Dan's gets smashed next. 'We're leaving, and you're coming with us. March.'

The men push them across the clearing and into the wood. Just then it starts to rain.

18

Once she's sure everyone's left, Fran steps out from behind the tree where she's been hiding. She's seen everything. She's scared, really scared. If she'd brought her mobile she'd have been able to call the police. But she didn't, so she can't. She's never felt more alone. And as for the boys ... it all depends on her now.

She'll give them a few minutes to get a bit further down the path before following. The campsite's a real mess – the boys' empty backpacks, sleeping bags and clothes lying on the ground, food packets and the fish they caught scattered around the empty kitbag, the boys' mobiles smashed to bits. How could everything have gone so wrong, and so fast? Her rucksack bouncing up and down on her back, she hurries into the woods after them.

The few drops of a moment ago have turned into a heavy downpour. Good. The rain hammering down full force will cover the sound of her footsteps as she rushes from one tree to the next after them, keeping out of sight.

Along the sheep track, all the way down the hill, then onto the path that runs beside the stream. Just before the footbridge she sees them turn off and begin to go uphill again. She waits.

On the other side of the stream she catches sight of the farmer, his tractor lumbering unevenly up and down on the far side of the field. If she runs really fast it'll only take a few minutes to go back, cross the footbridge, rush across his field, and shout up to him. Never mind the noise of his engine, or the loud music he's probably listening to on headphones – she'll stand right in front of his tractor and wave her arms until she gets him to stop. But then she'll have to explain everything. Will he believe her? Will he have a phone with him? Will there be a signal?

Has she even got the time? The boys have almost disappeared into the trees and she's in danger of losing them altogether. Most of all, she needs to know where they're being taken.

For several moments she stands in the driving rain, hesitating. What to do? What to do? *Some bad men have just kidnapped your friends, have they, little girl?* The farmer probably wouldn't believe a word of it. OK, forget the farmer. The best she can do is keep as close to the boys as possible and not let them out of her sight. She rushes to catch up.

Ten minutes later she sees them up ahead, crossing a stretch of moorland – completely open country, bordered by a wood. At once, she crouches down low in a hollow. The ground's wet and muddy, ankle-deep. With the rain lashing down on her, she remains out of sight. They must be making for the wood. Shoulders hunched in the gusting rain, the two men shove the boys forward every few steps. They plod their way over the marshland; around them the sheep scatter in every direction. Nessie looks too drenched and miserable to give chase. Finally they all disappear into the trees.

Fran stands up. Peering through the heavy curtain of rain she fixes in her mind the point where they entered between two silver birches – determined to keep it directly ahead of her. She'd like to give herself a good shake after being scrunched up on the sodden ground, but daren't delay. Stepping on grassy tussocks the better to avoid more marshy puddles and more mud, though it hardly matters now, she hurries after them. A few minutes later, she too enters the wood.

But there's no path anymore. Nothing but trees on all sides, trees and more trees. No rain, no wind. It's darker in here, very quiet and totally still. The ground's covered in pine needles and moss that's so spongy-soft her footsteps hardly make a sound. She goes a few steps, then stops.

This way? That way? She peers frantically from side to side. Where have they gone? Where? There's no sense in just blundering about. She stands quite motionless, and listens. Nothing. She listens harder. But all she can hear is the distant rain hammering onto the treetops overhead; around her the deep silence is broken only by the drip and splatter-patter of occasional raindrops on the leaves.

Then from far away … Yes! She'd recognise that bark anywhere. Nessie! Good girl! Fran sets off towards the sound. Moving quietly and quickly, she half-walks, half-runs, dodging again from tree to tree, pausing a moment then dashing forward again. In less than a couple of minutes, she's caught sight of them once more. She hunkers down next to a bush to let them get a little further ahead, then makes for another bush, a tree. She can see them quite clearly now. The men seem to know where they're going and keep shoving Dan and Steve, telling them to hurry up.

Then, quite abruptly, they come to a total stop.

Just in time she ducks out of sight behind a tree and peers round the side.

Shavehead's pulled out his knife.

She almost screams out loud. Surely he's not going to ... She presses herself so close up against the trunk she can almost taste the sodden stickiness of the bark, wet moss-slime against her face.

Next, she sees him pull out something else. The black plastic bag. He removes the wad of money, splits it in two and crams it in his pockets.

Wiping away the rainwater dripping from her hair into her eyes, she takes a deep breath. If things start to go totally bad, she's ready to—

With a quick slash of the knife he slices the plastic bag in two and hands one piece to Red Hair. He orders Dan to turn around, and blindfolds him with the strip of plastic, tying it at the back. Steve, too, is blindfolded.

They're turned round and round so they can't tell what direction they're going in.

Red Hair takes something out of his pocket. 'I knew this would come in handy.'

A moment later each boy has been gagged with a strip of duct tape.

'Get going,' orders Shavehead. 'Lucky it's raining, so there's no hikers wandering around. No danger anyone seeing what they shouldn't. Move it. You can hold onto our sticks.'

The procession moves awkwardly forward, Shavehead going ahead first with Steve stumbling behind and holding onto the broken branch. Red Hair follows, leading Dan. Fran lets them get ahead, then sets off. Progress is slow, which suits her. At this speed she'll have no problem keeping them in sight.

19

Steve feels the rain easing. He's so soaked through that he really doesn't give a toss – it could rain forever for all he cares. Things are just getting worse and worse, and he feels he's been holding onto this bit of tree branch and stumbling forward like a blind man for as long as he can remember, and at any moment his next step could take him over the edge of a cliff. All he knows is that they're no longer walking downhill and, having crossed a piece of flat ground that was probably a field, they've now come to tarmac or cement.

A road? Someone's garden? Their footsteps echo off nearby walls. Some kind of courtyard, maybe?

'That's far enough.'

Nessie is somewhere near, her nails click-clacking on the hard ground.

'I'll go check on Sonia and give her the heads-up about these two.' That's Kojak speaking. Then there's the sound of his footsteps walking away.

'Don't move,' says Elvis.

There's a creaking sound like rusty hinges. Most likely a door being pushed open, its bottom scraping the ground. Steve feels Nessie brush against him; her wet muzzle presses into his hand, a lick. He gives her a pat.

'In you go.' A hard shove in his back. Elvis again.

Steve lurches forward – and suddenly he's out of the rain. It feels chilly, and a bit damp. There's the smell of old hay. They must be at a farm, in one of the byres or sheds.

'Come here.'

He stumbles towards the sound of the man's voice. The floor's uneven and he nearly trips over some kind of gutter. He walks into an outstretched hand that's been held up flat, making him stop. He's gripped by the shoulder and forced down.

'Kneel.'

What? He tries to speak through his gag and it comes out as a grunt.

'Down on your knees, I said.'

Surely they're not going to behead him? They don't seem like terrorists.

He kneels.

'Sit up straight.'

Now he gets it – he's been made to kneel with his back against some kind of pillar. It feels solid, made of brick or stone.

'Hands behind your back.'

His arms are forced round the sides of the pillar.

'Hands together.' There's the sound of tape being wrapped round his wrists. 'That's you done. Now for your pal.'

Steve tries to pull, but the duct tape won't give an inch. He's stuck.

Where's Nessie? Steve can't feel her near him, can't hear the *clack-clack* of her paws. Nessie would chew through the tape in a minute – so long as it was meat-flavoured. But if the thug has brought some of the salami with him, she'll stick to him. She'll think it's Christmas and he's Santa.

And Fran? Did she really just up and leave them? Her stuff wasn't there so she must have. But she'd tidied the place up first, which was weird. Why bother? At least she's safe, wherever she is. If only they were all safe and—

'You're the smart one, I think.' It's Elvis, his voice really close like he's bending down in front of him, only inches away from his face.

Steve makes no response – that's what the smart one would do. He waits for what's coming next.

'Stay here and you'll stay alive. Kojak wanted to cut you back there in the caves. Permanently. Would've snuffed you and buried you out in the woods. Given it no more thought than stubbing out his fag. I talked him out of it. Understand?' The man grips him under the chin. Steve feels the man's breath and spit. 'Understand?'

He does his best to give a yes-sounding grunt, and a nod.

'You'd better. See, I'm your friend here. Your only friend. Better remember that.'

Steve manages another grunt, another nod.

'Right then.'

A moment later the door creaks open and then scrapes shut. Elvis has gone.

Is this how it's all going to end? Can't see, can't speak, sitting on a cement floor tied to a stone pillar? In his rain-sodden jacket, T-shirt and jeans, and getting colder by the minute, waiting for – what? His life can't stop now. There's so much to live for, so much to do; there are so many places to see, so many people to get to know. And there's Fran and ... everything. He grunts through the duct tape, as loud as he can, as furiously as he can. But that's all he can do – grunt. A moment later Dan grunts back. A few grunts pass back and forth between them. Then they stop. What's the point? The worst of it is that no one knows where they are. Even they don't know where they are.

20

Crouched low in the long grass that covers the hillside, Fran looks down to the farm where the boys have been taken. The rain's almost stopped, thank goodness. The place seems totally neglected, like it's been abandoned. No people or animals in sight, but maybe they've been inside, sheltering from the recent downpour. The farmhouse itself needs more than a few licks of paint; there are weeds growing out of the gutters and the TV aerial's lying flat on the roof, hanging on only by its cable. Patches of bare cement show through the walls like grey mould on cheese. Same with the outbuildings that are grouped in a horseshoe shape around the yard, with the farmhouse at the top and, at the bottom, entrance gates set wide open, then a farm track that'll probably lead to the main road. An old tractor stands rusting in one corner next to an unhooked trailer. There's a sleek, shiny car parked outside the farmhouse door. They keep all that money hidden in the cave, drive what looks like a spanking new Mercedes, and yet they live in this dump?

She watches Shavehead go into a shed next to the farmhouse, Nessie trotting along beside him. So much for man's best friend being loyal. That dog's loyal only to her stomach. Having shoved the boys into another shed and left them there, Red Hair's now come out again. He crosses the farmyard and goes into the same building as Shavehead.

Steve and Dan? Have they been hurt so badly they can't move? Or has something much worse happened to them?

She daren't even think about it. She has to *do* something, and do it now.

The farmer. She can tell him where the boys are being kept and it's an emergency and ...

But could she find her way back through the wood? Or she could try to get down to the road and stop a car and—

There's an engine sound coming from behind her, from above. The whup-whup-whup's getting louder and louder, and within seconds its churning roar is almost directly overhead. A helicopter, and it's flying so low she has to put her hands over her ears. She watches it circle above the farm, dropping in height, the long grass on the slope between her and the buildings flattening in its downdraught. As it descends the last twenty feet before settling to land in the yard, Shavehead comes back out of the shed, a woman with him. They're having to shield their faces from the air being gusted and whirled around them. They remain close to the shed wall, letting the blades slow down before approaching.

Finally the chopper door opens, a small ladder appears and a man clambers down. Looks like a businessman – dark suit, shirt and tie, attaché case. The others go across to greet him. They shake hands. Clearly he's important. Meanwhile the pilot's stepped down from the other side. The blades have come to a complete stop. It's quiet again. Fran can hear sheep in a nearby field. It's as if that helicopter-roar ripped the sky wide open, and now everything is sealed up again – back to normal.

Except for Steve and her brother. They're prisoners and she'll have to rescue them – there's no one else. Now that a helicopter's shown up there's no time to go for help. She really is on her own.

The two men, the woman and Mr Businessman have gone into the farmhouse. They're adults so they'll probably sit-sit-sit and talk-talk-talk. Suits her. The farmyard's empty.

It'll take her less than ten minutes to get down there, but she'll need to be light on her feet. She pulls off her rucksack and dumps it on the ground. All she'll really need is . . .

She rips off the duct tape and plastic wrapping. She lets the gun rest in her hand, feeling its weight, its balance, its solid grip. Then gets to her feet and points it at the farm. 'Bang!' she says under her breath. But is it loaded?

She'll find out when she pulls the trigger.

21

It sounds like a giant dentist is drilling the sky and his drill's getting louder and nearer every second. A whirling-churning roar that Steve knows can only be a helicopter. Special Forces or SAS come to rescue them?

If only.

The chopper's suddenly right overhead – the whole building's shaking now. Worse than a hurricane threatening to rip off the roof or an earthquake tearing houses apart like they're made of paper, throwing cars about like toys. The walls, the pillar, the stone floor – everything's shuddering.

It sounds like the helicopter's landed right outside their shed door. Maybe it really has come to rescue them?

Dream on.

The engine's whining down and he hears the separate swishing strokes as the blades slow to a standstill. Switch off the hurricane, the earthquake. It's calm again. The roof's still in place, the walls are still standing – and they're still prisoners.

A door slams. Voices, lots of them. Steve strains and strains, but can't make out what's being said. Is the helicopter here to take the men away, leaving him and Dan behind – gagged, blindfolded and tied to their pillars? Stuck here until somebody finds them?

Or until nobody finds them?

And what about Fran? Will he ever see her again?

Everything's gone quiet – deadly quiet.

If he had superpowers there'd be no problem. He'd simply grip the pillar in his arms, and pull-pull-pull super-hard, wrenching it out from the floor. Only, that might bring down the roof. But if he really did have superpowers he'd just reach up and hold the roof in place with one hand. Really, the problem's not about being trapped here – but about not having superpowers.

Mind you, if he really did have superpowers he wouldn't be tied to this stupid pillar in the first place.

The duct tape won't stretch, won't loosen. It's strong – stronger than him, anyway. He gives Dan another grunt. Dan grunts back.

At least Fran's safe. Wherever she is.

Elvis is no friend of theirs, no matter what he says. Kojak's even worse. He looks worse too. Elvis at least looks like a normal grown-up, Kojak's like a grown-up grown wrong. Wrong outside and inside, you can feel it. Still smiling his broken-glass smile when he was threatening to kill Nessie. Adults have superpowers, sort of. But the more powerful they are, the more they seem to waste them. If he ever does get superpowers, he won't waste them, that's for sure.

Suddenly there's the sound of the door creaking open.

22

Keeping herself bent low in the long grass, Fran zigzags her way down the slope. After a dozen metres, she pauses. Sticks her head up for a moment, looks around, sees no one. Zigzags a dozen more. Stops again. Looks round. The sun's beginning to come out; there's the smell of wet grass. A flock of birds sweeps past, chattering as they go. She waits. Sees no one. Zigzags down to the last stretch where the ground's flat. There's a fence up ahead. Almost down on her hands and knees, she hurries across to within a metre of the barbed wire. Beyond is an open field. Lying flat on the damp grass she takes a good look round, scanning in every direction.

No one.

Is she sure?

She waits a moment more.

Yes, quite sure.

On her elbows, she crawls under the bottom wire.

The fence now behind her, she's instantly up on her feet and running over to the farm wall.

She stops, gets her breath back. No one about. Definitely no one. They must still be sit-sitting, talk-talking in the farmhouse.

From now on she needs to be quick, but quiet. She daren't make a noise.

Keeping close against the wall she creeps down to the bottom corner of the horseshoe-shaped farmyard, lowering her head whenever she comes to a window – not that it matters much, the windows are boarded up.

She pauses again to get her breath, to calm herself.

So far, so good – but now is when things will get dangerous. When she sticks her head round the corner, she'll be visible to anyone in the yard, to anyone coming up the farm track. OK, quick as she can.

Head round . . .

The farmyard seems quiet: helicopter in the middle, old tractor against a wall, Merc outside the house. Not a person in sight.

. . . and back.

The boys are in a shed on the other side of the yard – but which door was it?

Head round again . . .

The middle two, she's sure. They're both painted green, both look old and battered.

. . . and back.

Suppose it's locked? Only one way to find out.

Head round . . .

Clear.

She sprints past the silent helicopter to the other side of the yard. She tries the door handle. It opens. She goes in.

It's pitch dark. Totally. No daylight even. Without thinking she fumbles for a light switch, finds it just inside the door.

Next moment, the shed's blazing with light. So very bright. Banks of floodlights, it seems like. Dozens of full-strength lamps have been strung on pulleys to hang above four enormous tables that take up most of the shed. The tables are covered with row upon row of plant pots and plant trays, hundreds and hundreds of them. It's like a garden centre – a secret garden centre where the windows have been boarded up to keep out daylight. Old plant leaves and earth lie strewn on the floor.

Loudly as she dares, she calls out, 'Steve? Dan?'

No response. All she can hear are mice. Lots of them. They're scrabbling and scratching, scuttling and squeaking. She doesn't like mice.

She's snapped off the lights and is about to leave when she hears a door nearby creak open.

23

'Here are the two small problems I mentioned.'

It's Kojak.

Then Elvis speaks. 'But we'll need to . . .'

As they don't come any closer, Steve can't make out much more. Just that they're talking, talking, talking.

Then he hears Nessie coming across to him, her paws clacking on the stone floor. Painfully, he eases himself forward. It's good to feel her nuzzling him, licking his face. She's settled down next to him, all furry and wet-nosey, which makes him feel a bit better.

Then a voice he's not heard before, a man's. 'They can describe you . . .'

Steve starts grunting at them. Pleading grunts. Angry grunts. *No . . . No . . .*

'. . . they can talk to the cops, and . . .'

Won't talk . . . Won't talk . . . He shakes his head till it nearly falls off.

A woman's voice chimes in. 'Kids always blab. Can't help it.'

Won't blab . . . Won't blab . . .

The man again. 'You've a couple of days to tidy up the loose ends. You'll do what you need to.'

Do what you need to! Steve's seen enough films to know what that means.

24

As there's only a thin plasterboard partition separating this part of the shed from the part next door, where the boys are being kept, Fran can hear most of what's being said. If she can hear them, they can probably hear *her*. She stops moving, stops breathing.

'... take them with us?'

'... no one'll come to the farm for weeks. Could just leave them here and ...'

'... same as killing them, but worse.'

'... or else make it look like suicide.'

'Suicide? A couple of schoolkids?' The woman's got a loud, snappy voice like a bad-tempered schoolteacher on a bad-tempered day. Mrs Bad-temper keeps talking. 'Either it's killing them and burying the bodies in the woods or—'

Killing them? Killing Steve and Dan?

'No killing kids – I saw enough of that in Helmand.'

Suddenly Fran knows she's about to sneeze. A tickle that gets ticklier and ticklier.

Her hand clamped over her nose. Still tickling. Hold it ... hold it ... hold it ...

The sneeze passes.

The door's slammed shut. They've left. She hears them walking away, talking as they go. Still arguing. But not a sound from through the partition. Steve and Dan? It's gone totally quiet. Have they been taken away already?

They talked about *killing* them.

No sounds from outside. What she doesn't want is Nessie coming up to her, barking a big hello.

And so she eases open the door into the farmyard. Just an inch.

Then another inch.

She peers out through the gap.

The yard's empty like before. The helicopter, the old tractor, the shiny Merc. Nothing else. No one. They must have all gone back into the farmhouse.

A few seconds later she's in the next-door shed. Smaller, but just as cluttered with plant pots and—

Steve and Dan! Still blindfolded and gagged, they're both tied to pillars. They're still alive, thank goodness.

Steve's nearer to her. Keeping her voice low, she whispers, 'It's me. Fran.' She slides the blindfold off his head. In his eyes there's a look of utter amazement.

Grunt-grunt.

'We've got to be quiet. They could come back at any minute. Now for your gag. One quick pull?'

Grunt-grunt.

'It'll hurt. Not a sound, remember.'

Grunt-grunt.

She can see he's tensed his jaw to stop himself crying out, but, just to be sure, she's ready to clamp a hand over his mouth. With one hand she takes good hold of the strip of duct tape, and places the other on his shoulder to steady herself. She leans close to him and whispers: 'One, two . . .'

Then the strongest, most sudden tug she can manage.

'Yeowwww—' He immediately grits his teeth tight shut. He's holding his breath. She gives his shoulder an encouraging squeeze. Then a moment later he breathes out. He's one big smile.

'Thank you, thank you. But, Fran, how did you ... where have you ...? It's like a miracle!'

'*Shh!* No time to talk. They might come back any moment. Got to get you loose.' Going behind the pillar, she starts picking at the tape holding his wrists – not so easy without a knife. She works on a corner with her thumbnail.

'*Grunt-grunt-grunt*,' says Dan.

'Be there in a moment, little brother.' But the duct tape's stuck and stuck hard. 'Just hold on.' It's so difficult to get a grip, and the tape's so strong. At last, an edge starts to lift. It takes her only a couple of seconds to unwind the rest.

'*Grunt-grunt-grunt-grunt-grunt.*'

'Coming, Dan.' She stands up.

A minute later Dan's free as well.

'Ready, everyone?' She goes towards the door. 'We've got to get out of here – and fast!'

25

Steve cracks the door open a few inches to check out the yard. The rain must've stopped while they were tied up in the shed. Clear blue skies now, hardly a cloud. Perfect weather for escaping! Even better, there's no one in sight. But no Nessie either. Where is she? They can't just leave her.

Fran nudges him in the back and points to the bottom of the yard. 'On you go!'

'But Nessie—'

'We've got to go *now*!' She shoves him. 'Fast as you can.'

'But they might—'

'Come on!' Fran rushes out the door and Dan goes hammering after her.

He can't just abandon Nessie.

He sees Fran and Dan disappear round the corner of the yard. OK then. If he does get away safely, he'll come back for her. Somehow.

He's hardly gone a couple of steps when he hears the farmhouse door opening and sees Kojak coming out. He's already ducking into the shed next door. Everything's happening too fast.

Pitch darkness. The sweat's running down his back. His heart's hammering. *You'll do what you need to.*

He hears the door of the shed where they'd been tied up creak open. Then Kojak's rushed back out, shouting and yelling. 'They've escaped!' Steve can hear the anger in the man's voice. The rage. 'You and you – take the track in case they head to the road, me and Elvis'll take the fields.' The man is in a total fury.

There's the sound of running footsteps.

Then total silence.

Suddenly Fran's at the door. 'They've gone. Come on.'

'Come on where?'

'The one place they'll never look.'

26

Seconds later they've climbed into the helicopter. It's a four-seater – two front and two back. They lie down on the floor between the two rows, out of sight. No one looking up from the ground will be able to see them.

'But, Fran, what if the pilot comes and takes off?'

'Then we escape in style, little brother!'

'I'm going to see if Ness—'

Suddenly there's shouting and yelling in the yard. Kojak, Elvis and the rest of the gang are back. Luckily the helicopter doors are mostly glass so Steve hardly needs to raise his head more than a few inches to see what's going on. Kojak's raging, screaming his head off and kicking open all the shed doors. They're looking behind the tractor and trailer, under the car, checking everywhere. Everyone's screaming their head off apart from a guy in a suit who's standing with his arms folded, looking on and doing nothing. Steve hears him tell the others, 'I'm leaving soon. This is your mess, tidy it up.'

A moment later, someone's come out of the farmhouse, carrying a large cardboard box like it's groceries. He's walking down towards the chopper, and as he passes the suit he calls out, 'I'll be getting her started. Good to go in five.'

Steve whispers, 'Keep down, everyone, not a sound. Pilot's coming.'

The helicopter rocks a little to one side as the pilot clambers up the steps. He takes his seat, only inches in front of where the three of them are hiding. He places the box on the front passenger seat. Whistling under his breath, he gets himself settled and buckled in. He takes a piece of chewing gum out of his pocket, unwraps it and pops it into his mouth. He moves from whistling into humming as he flicks levers, taps dials, presses buttons. The chopper gives a shudder. The engine starts up. Slowly, slowly the rotor blades begin to turn. A *swish-sweep* that gets louder and louder as they pick up speed, turning faster and faster.

The noise is soon deafening. Steve daren't raise

his head to check what's happening outside. He can hear what sounds like an argument. One side of it, anyway. Kojak's yelling to be heard above the roar from the rotors, but Steve can't make out what he's saying.

The cabin's vibrating and juddering. The guy in the suit will soon be climbing on board and then they'll probably take off. The engine's whining fit to burst, the rotor noise is deafening. Any minute now . . .

What about Nessie? And *where* will they fly off to?

Steve can't believe what Fran does next. She stands up, reaches over to the pilot in his seat and yells into his ear: 'Never mind your passenger. Lift her up now. NOW!'

'What? Who're you? Where did you come from?'

'Feel that? It's a gun.' She's holding it to the pilot's head, pressing the barrel just behind his ear.

The man glances quickly round. 'But you're just a kid. A girl—'

'A girl with a gun, and I'm pointing it right at you. Let's go!'

Outside, the others have seen what's happening.

They're staring up at the cockpit like they can't believe their eyes – totally gobsmacked!

Steve and Dan stand up.

Fran's yelling above the engine noise: 'Everyone get strapped in!'

The boys climb into the back passenger seats and buckle up. Keeping the gun trained on the pilot, she pushes the package onto the floor and takes the empty seat.

Over the roar of the engine and the scream of the turning rotors the pilot yells at Fran, and Fran yells at the pilot. Then, using both hands like they do in the cop films, she sticks the gun right into his face. He raises his hand as if to say: *OK, OK.*

Next instant he's vanished. Jumped clear out through his open door and landed on the ground, rolling over.

Fran turns to Steve and yells, 'His seat – take it!'

Steve stares back at her. She's expecting *him* to fly the helicopter? She's joking. She must be.

Once he's clambered over, she hands him a set of headphones and puts on a pair herself. Steve can hear her voice now, speaking to him loud and clear. 'Maybe it's a bit like an Xbox. That lever . . .' She's pointing to what could be a joystick. 'That probably lifts it up. Shut the door, Steve, and let's go.'

As she talks, she keeps glancing out through the windscreen – and whenever anyone starts coming nearer the chopper she points her gun at them.

'Come on, Steve, let's go! Go! GO!'

'You're kidding!'

'We stay and we're dead. Simple as that. This is our only chance. We won't go high.'

'We won't go at all. No need. With you holding the gun on them we can walk right out of here and—'

But can they? Steve can see the gang have divided into two and are coming across the yard, approaching the chopper. Kojak, the pilot and the businessman on his side, Elvis and the woman on Fran's – and she's having to swivel from one to the other to keep the gun pointing at them. The helicopter blades are whirling round so fast the criminals' hair and clothes are getting wind-blasted and they've to struggle to keep from being blown off their feet. But still they keep on coming. Nearer. Nearer. A few more steps, and one side and then the other will have reached the chopper doors.

Fran's right. This is their only chance. He clambers into the pilot's seat, takes hold of the lever. Then hesitates. He can't just . . .

Then Fran leans forward, slaps her hand down on top of his and presses hard.

27

Suddenly the cockpit lurches violently to the left, then even more violently to the right.

Very slightly Steve eases back his hand and everything steadies. But not by much. At once Fran is pressing down again on top – this time the left side of the chopper actually rises up a few inches, the cockpit tilts ... then tilts back down again. Slamming onto the tarmac, slamming down hard. They must have been a few inches up in the air!

Outside, everyone's rushed backwards to get clear.

Steve slides the lever again. The chopper rises a couple of metres, very, very shakily. For a moment they seem to be hanging in mid-air, jerking from side to side like they're swinging on the end of a very long rope.

He shifts his hand for a split second, trying to get a better grip of the lever – and again they come slamming down hard, with a massive *THUMP* onto the ground. Only the safety belt holds him in his seat.

A voice comes through the headphones: 'OK, you win. See, we're pulling back.'

Kojak? Steve looks out the windscreen and, sure enough, the gang have gathered at the top of the yard in front of the farmhouse. Speaking into some kind of phone or walkie-talkie that must be connected to the pilot's headset is Kojak. The man's staring straight at him.

'No need to kill yourselves. Taking off's easy, so I'm told. Just working a lever. Landing's the problem. And believe me, sonny-boy, it's a big, big problem.'

Right enough.

'So here's what we'll do. Nothing's really happened so far. No one's really got hurt. Agreed?'

What about him and Dan being shoved around, blindfolded and tied up with duct tape? What about that threat: *You'll do what you need to?* But Steve answers him anyway: 'Agreed.'

'Right, here's the deal – you climb down from the helicopter and you get to walk away. Like nothing's happened. You forget you ever saw us and we'll forget we ever saw you. Then everyone gets back to their normal lives. You, me, all of us. OK?'

Fran's shaking her head. She's reached forward to put her hand on his, like she wants to make him press down on the lever again.

This time he stops her, grabbing her hand.

'Give us a couple of minutes,' Steve says into the mouthpiece.

'Take your time. We don't want to lose the helicopter, and no one wants you to crash-land, explode into flames and burn to death. Which you will.'

He's right again.

So that Kojak can't hear what they say, Steve and Fran take off their headphones. Then, over the roar of the engine, they start yelling at each other.

'It's a trick, Steve. Must be.'

'Because he sounded too friendly all of a sudden? But helicopters are really expensive and—'

'For them, us getting killed is the best thing that could happen. On top of that, they'd probably get insurance money for the chopper.'

'But—'

'Think about it, Steve. We'd be the bad kids who ran away from home, stole a helicopter to go joyriding and crashed it. We'd have got what we deserved, and all their problems would be solved. So it must be a trick.'

'Then why not just let us do it?'

'I don't know. But, trust me – they'd prefer us dead. They *want* us dead.'

He glances out the windscreen to check all the gang are still up at the farmhouse, and sees them standing in a line as if it was a bus queue – Kojak in his denim biker jacket, red-haired Elvis, the pilot the businessman and the woman.

'We need to think, Steve – and think fast.'

Behind them, Dan is still strapped in his seat. He's staring straight ahead at nothing, probably near-deafened by the relentless roar of the engine and the churning blades, and looking pretty sick after all the thumping and bumping about.

A trick? thinks Steve. *What kind of trick? What could they be—*

'The package! It must be!' Fran yells suddenly. 'The pilot brought it and . . . Take care of this.' Then Steve can't hear what she's saying any more as she gives him the gun and reaches down for the cardboard box. She rips it open.

28

Cue CSI – the carton's full of sealed see-through plastic packets. White powder.

Fran puts her arm round Steve's neck and pulls him close again so they can speak.

'Drugs,' she yells. 'They don't want to lose them. Must be thousands, hundreds of thousands of pounds' worth here.'

'And they won't want any trace of drugs found at the crash site. Not that we're going to crash, that is,' Steve adds quickly.

Again Fran's pressing down on his hand to slide the lever. 'Maybe we can land it OK? Worth a try. They'll not let us walk away, that's for sure. Not now.'

Steve's still thinking things through. Stay, and they're dead for certain. Take off, and they're dead only maybe.

Suddenly Fran's pressed down on the lever.

With a sickening lurch the chopper pitches to the left, nearly toppling over. Then there's a roar from the engine and they've shot up into the air – twenty, thirty metres. Feels like a hundred.

'Christ, Fran! We can't—' He jams on his headphones again. 'What the hell are you doing, Fran? This is crazy!'

He looks down to the tops of the shed roofs and beyond. So very far below, he sees fields, the river, a road. If they drop suddenly and thump back down onto the ground from this height . . .

Suddenly they're freefalling out the sky to stop only a few metres above the ground. For several seconds they hang there in mid-air, swinging from side to side like they're on the worst rollercoaster ride ever. Then the chopper steadies.

'I think I'm getting the idea, Steve.'

'You think? You're going to get us killed first.'

Kojak's voice cuts in. 'I agree. Ease the chopper back down. We'll all stay here, I promise. Get landed, get out and you can all walk away. I give you my word.'

Easy as that?

'I'll even add a thousand in cash for each of you. Call it a bonus.'

Fran's shaking her head. Steve feels her hand tensing on his, steadying it.

Then he has an idea. A great idea. First, though, a counter-offer to show Kojak who's in charge. 'Here's a better deal. We leave here – with *five* thousand each.'

'Agreed.'

'And Nessie.'

'Agreed. The dog's all yours.'

Now for the clincher. 'Right, Kojak, we want the Merc brought to the side of the chopper, doors open, key in the ignition and engine running. Fifteen thousand on the front seat. We want all of you back inside the farmhouse, and you're to stay there. Then, and only then, do we come down. We'll drive straight off. And no tricks – we're armed, remember.'

Fran gives Steve a big thumbs-up and a smile to die for. He knows that both she and Dan get to drive cars round the forecourt of their dad's garage, and he's driven round there himself a few times.

'Agreed. Now bring her down.'

'Slowly, Fran. Slowly.'

They drop a foot, then stop . . . a little more . . . a little more … then *THUMP!* They're back on the ground. Shuddering and shaking, but they're here. Going by car'll be a piece of cake after this!

Or it should be …

But nothing's happening. The whole gang are still *outside* the farmhouse, not standing in an orderly queue any more, but huddled together, talking. Arguing, it looks like. Nessie's running around them, barking and barking.

Steve feels himself getting angry – really, really angry. Here they are, ordinary kids wanting to get on with their ordinary lives, while the adults shout at each other, as usual, and they can only look on and wait – as usual.

Wait around long enough and you get turned into an adult and spend your time shouting and arguing too. Is that what's meant by growing up? He feels like telling them, *Waste your own lives if you want to, but don't waste ours.* But they wouldn't listen; they never do.

Then things start to happen.

Elvis has walked away. He's got into the Merc. He's driving it down to the chopper. Good. He parks it. He gets out. He leaves the front doors open. Good. Steve can see small puffs of smoke coming from the exhaust, so he knows the engine's still running. Elvis returns to join the rest of the gang. Good. All good so far.

A few minutes later, Kojak comes strolling down towards them, carrying what looks like a supermarket bag in one hand and a length of rope in the other, leading Nessie. He reaches them and glances up into the cockpit, smiling that broken smile of his. He lifts the bag higher. 'Fifteen thousand in fifties,' he says, across their headphones. He leans into the car and tosses the bag onto the front seat.

Once he's gone back inside the farmhouse they can climb down from the chopper and drive off. They'll leave the sorry grown-ups to shout at each other and drug each other and obsess about money for the rest of their greedy lives.

Can it really be going so easily? Kojak's too cruel-looking – Steve doesn't trust his cold eyes and that smile of his. No matter what he promises, no matter what he does, Steve can't believe he's going to just let them—

'Your dog.' Kojak's slipped the rope off Nessie's collar and crouches down beside her, feeding her some meat out of his pocket. The blow-down from the churning chopper blades makes his denim jacket billow. 'Come on down, sonny-boy, and I'll hand her over.'

No, Steve definitely doesn't trust him. Not an inch. He's going to do something, something really, really bad. To them, to Nessie. Because that's the kind of man he is. Can't help himself.

Dan's fiddling with his buckle, ready to lean over and open his door.

'Wait, Dan. Not yet.'

Steve speaks into the mouthpiece. 'Leave Nessie and go inside the farmhouse.'

Fran joins in. 'That's what we agreed. Now do it.'

'Then we'll climb down, and not before. Like I said.'

Kojak continues stroking Nessie while glancing up at them and smiling his cruel smile.

'What's happening?' Dan cries. 'What do we do now?'

Steve only knows what they *don't* do – they don't climb out of the chopper. Not yet, anyway.

He glances at Fran. She's very tense. She shouts into her mouthpiece, 'You bastard! Let that dog go and stick to what we agreed.'

'Not very polite, are you?' says Kojak. 'If I had a daughter like you, I'd make her wash her mouth out with soap.' He continues stroking Nessie's head, continues smiling.

Suddenly Steve's had it. Before, he was angry. Now he's furious. Utterly furious with this *grown-up* who can't keep his word for even two minutes. He aims the gun right at him and yells, 'Get back up to the house – or I'll shoot!'

Instead, Kojak reaches into his pocket ...

29

'You bastard!' Fran screams. 'Touch our dog and—'

Casually, Kojak wipes the blade of his knife on Nessie's fur. 'Language, little lady. Now open the door, and climb down one at a time.'

Meanwhile, Elvis and the others have started to step towards the helicopter.

Steve can feel his finger curling round the trigger. Would he manage to hit him? Suppose he hit Nessie instead.

His hands are shaking like they're getting multiple electric shocks. Kojak's staring back at him. Not quite so confident-looking, but he's not moving away either.

OK, the man's asking for it. It'll serve him right. Gun gripped in both hands, Steve crouches, squints his eyes to look along the barrel. He takes aim, but shakily, the barrel waving all over the place.

Beside him, he hears Fran unbuckling herself and getting to her feet. But he won't let her stop him. No one's going to stop him. Kojak's right in his sights now.

'You want this?' says Fran.

'What?' Steve glances quickly round at her.

But she's talking into her mouthpiece. 'You want it, Kojak?' She's holding up one of the drug packets, waving it.

That gets the thug's attention.

Next moment, Fran's ripped the packet open. She holds it out the chopper window and shakes it out into the swirling downdraught from the blades, to get carried away on the rush of wind. The bag's empty in seconds.

'Stop! Stop!' screams Kojak.

Fran doesn't stop. She lifts up plastic bag number two, starts waving it around.

'STOP! STOP! STOP!' The criminal has taken a step nearer the chopper. 'You want your dog, you throw down our box.'

Steve reaches for the carton at his feet. Fran lays her hand on his shoulder to stop him, and shakes her head. She rips open the bag, leans out the window and empties it into the fierce wind. Second bag gone.

Kojak takes another step. Nessie gets up on her hind legs, putting her paws on his chest like it's all the best game ever.

'Right then, Kojak,' says Fran. 'Do what I tell you. Tie Nessie to the car. Go back ten paces and I'll throw down the next bag.'

'Make it five.'

'Make it fifteen, Kojak – or that bag'll be blowing in the wind as well.'

'All right. All right. Here's your dog.' He loops the rope round the car's front bumper and starts to walk towards the farmhouse.

At a nod from Fran, Steve leans out and throws one of the bags onto the ground. Poor Nessie, he sees, is frantic. She's so very close to the chopper, only a few metres away from the high-pitched rotors, and the downdraught's battering her like a hurricane. Roped to the Merc's bumper, she's terrified, barking wildly, jumping up on her hind legs, tugging, tugging to wrench herself free.

Kojak has come to where the rest of the gang are gathered. 'That's your ten paces.'

'Another ten, another bag. That means the lot of you.'

The criminals turn and begin walking. Their ten paces take them almost to the farmhouse. Steve feels great watching these grown-ups doing exactly what they're told, like a bunch of puppets, with Fran and him pulling their strings.

She nods to him and he tosses out another packet. All's going well. This really might—

Nessie! She's shaken her rope free of the car and started back up towards Kojak and the others.

NO!

Kojak puts up his hands, like he's saying it's not him who called her. Then he bends down, picks up a stone and throws it at the dog. She yelps.

Steve's half out of the cockpit when Fran grabs hold of him.

'Now, get into the farmhouse, all of you,' she shouts into the mouthpiece. 'And close the door.'

Steve tosses down another packet. Only three left.

And into the farmhouse they go – the whole gang, like a flock of sheep being herded by an invisible dog. The farmhouse door's pulled shut behind them. Just like magic! Better, even! A few seconds later, he sees

Kojak and Elvis standing at the window. Exactly where they should be – in their sheep pen! This is going to work. It's really going to work!

Fran pushes aside her mouthpiece. 'We've got to be quick. Out of the chopper, down the steps, grab Nessie and into the car. No stopping for anything. Right, Steve, open your door. Dan—'

They look round to see Dan struggling with his seat belt. He's tugging at it, wrenching it. 'Jammed, it's jammed!'

30

'For God's sake, Dan!' Steve yells at the top of his voice. Then he sees the look on Dan's face, the utter terror, and stops himself. He didn't mean to scare him, but he must've sounded even worse than his dad. 'Sorry, sorry, Dan. I'm not yelling at *you* – it's just because of the engine noise. Let's see what's wrong and I'll fix it.' He takes the buckle in his hand. 'See, it's the same as a seat belt in a car. Easy-peasy. No worries, we'll be out of here in no time.'

But he knows they won't. Dan's buckle really *is* jammed.

Fran's shouting into the mouthpiece. 'Get back inside the house, the lot of you!'

Steve looks up to see the farmhouse door has opened and Kojak's now standing in the doorway. She's right – they'll have to be super-fast. The instant the three of them step down from the chopper the whole gang'll make a rush towards them, hoping to grab them before they can drive off.

157

'Plenty more plastic bags here,' shouts Fran. 'Get yourself back inside, Kojak, or I'll let the wind have the lot. Same for the ones on the ground.'

'You've only got three left.' Through his headpiece, Steve hears the taunt and sneer in the thug's voice. He keeps wrestling with Dan's buckle, but it's jammed solid. Hopeless. Maybe if Dan slides out from under the belt?

'And here's one of them,' he hears Fran tell them. She's ripped it open and holds it out her door. The powder's snatched by the fierce gust and is gone almost immediately. 'Back into the house or you'll have none left.'

The other packets are lying on the ground, within easy reach. If need be, Steve knows he can jump down and retrieve them.

Kojak lifts up his hands. 'OK, little lady. You're a tough nut, all right. I'm going back inside. Leave the rest of the packets lying where they are, and get the hell out of our lives.'

Once again the farmhouse door's pulled shut.

Fran turns round. 'Is he free yet?'

'Just about.'

Dan slides out, finally.

'Right, everyone ready? Steve, you grab Nessie and the two of you get in the back of the car. Dan, you come into the front with me. I'll drive. Everybody ready? OK, one, two, *three*!'

Then they're out the chopper, down on the ground, running bent over in the high wind. Steve's calling Nessie. 'Biscuits! Biscuits!' She comes, she jumps up. He grabs her, drags her to the car. He's reaching for the rear door handle when ... he hears the farmhouse door opening.

'We gotta go!' he yells.

He shoves Nessie into the car, then glances back only to see that Kojak's still just standing there, arms folded. Not moving. What's going on? Why's he not rushing down towards them?

Fran's got in behind the wheel, she's adjusting her seat so her feet can reach the pedals.

Suddenly Elvis, the pilot and the businessman come tearing round the bottom corner of the yard, racing towards the car. At the farmyard entrance the woman's swinging the gate closed. There's no way out.

'Back to the chopper!' yells Steve. Bundling Nessie in his arms, he pulls her out of the car, turns and races

over to the chopper, throwing her up into the cockpit. He clambers up the steps. A moment later everyone's in. The doors are slammed shut.

'Belts on!' Fran screams. She reaches for the big lever again. The chopper shudders violently. Through the windscreen they can see Elvis being almost blown off his feet and forced to scramble backwards. So, too, the businessman and the woman. 'Hold on tight, everyone!'

Next, they've shot up into the air, straight up like a rocket.

31

Within seconds they're well above the farm, and still climbing. The cockpit's shaking, vibrating, throwing them violently from side to side.

'Easy, Fran, easy ...'

As they go higher and higher, the view through the windscreen of the ever-smaller farm and the countryside slipping further and further below reminds Steve of zooming out from a Google map. Except this is real. This is *scary*.

'Those bastards!' Fran's nearly in tears. 'They must have gone out the back door and crept down behind the sheds. And now *this*! I don't know if I can—'

There's a violent jolt to the right.

'Must be these pedals.' She nods down at her feet. Two pedals. 'Seems I hardly need to touch them.' She nudges lightly with her right foot and the chopper lurches to the right. She lifts her foot and it steadies again. Then she gives the left pedal a nudge and the chopper lurches to the left. Nessie's trembling all over.

Looking down they can see the farm, the woods, fields, the river glinting with flecks of sunlight, a road.

'What's that stick thing?' asks Steve, pointing to a lever with a small button on the top.

'I don't know,' says Fran. 'Let's find out.'

'Really gently though, like with the pedals.'

'You don't need to tell me!' she snaps back. Then she gives him a scared-looking smile. 'Sorry, Steve, but . . .'

'It's OK. I understand. Forget it.'

'I know how to go up, how to go down and how to go sideways. So this button thing must be to make us go forward. It must be.' She looks at Steve. 'You think?'

'It's all yours, Fran. Go for it.'

At once, the front of the chopper lifts slightly, then lurches forward, and they're no longer above the farm. Immediately, the countryside beneath seems to slip behind them as if the Google map's been wrenched away.

'Too fast,' Fran cries out. 'The controls are super-sensitive, like on a touchscreen, but worse. Hardly need to press.'

More fields, another wood, some houses here and

there. A road with a red car travelling along it and a blue van coming behind that's going to overtake any moment. But already they're beyond them both, racing forward, racing across the sky!

Then Dan shouts to them from the back seat. 'But where are we going?'

No one answers. Fran's full attention is taken up with trying to keep the chopper in the air and fly in a straight line. Field after field disappears behind them, then a small village, a road, another road, a wood, a hill. They're flying on and on.

Suddenly Steve wishes he was back home, sharing his Tuesday pizza with Nessie – wishes it so much. He pictures his dad snoring on the couch; there's crap on the telly and his mum talking through it like always. Afterwards he'll go upstairs to his room. His own room, back to his normal, everyday—

Mr Doom puts in another tuppence-worth. 'And when we get there, we've still got Thor to deal with.'

Thor and his Vikings. Steve had forgotten all about them. Not any more.

'That cyber-slimebag?' he shouts. 'After what we've

been through, Thor's *nothing*. He's a creep, a total wimp hiding behind his computer screen because he's too frightened to show his face. He's a fart in a trance – and I'll blast him! Blast him good!' Before he knows it, he's started waving the gun around.

'STOP IT!' yells Fran.

He stops. Just as well, another moment and he might have pulled the trigger in his excitement.

'Sorry.' He shrugs and puts the gun back in his pocket.

Without taking her eyes from the windscreen, Fran shouts, 'Don't worry, little brother, we'll sort Thor. Sort him so totally there'll be nothing left of him.'

A few minutes later, Dan shouts, 'There's McDowell's chimney and the playing fields! We're nearly home!'

If only.

Fran glances down at the ground far below. 'Now for the hard bit.'

32

Neither Steve nor Dan say anything. But everyone's thinking the same thing. They can't keep flying on and on forever. They've got to land somewhere. They've got to land *somehow*.

They're passing within fifty metres of the timber yard chimney, its smoke billowing out into the clear sky, when a beeping noise starts up in the cockpit. It's an irritating sound, but they can't see anything wrong. No flashing lights come on, and Fran's sure the chopper's handling feels the same. Maybe it's an on-board sensor to detect that they're flying over a built-up area now, warning them to be careful – to watch out for church spires, tower blocks and the like? Fran ignores it. What else can she do? She has enough to think about.

She takes them in a very ragged and bumpy circle round the outskirts of town. Where to land? They discuss it. Fran and Steve do, that is. Dan's turned a bit green with all the swerving and lurching. Nessie's just staring straight ahead – she's one big tremble-and-shake from the tip of her nose to the end of her tail, like she's in shock. Steve tries patting and stroking to calm her, but she doesn't even notice. Then, for one moment, she catches his eye – and he can see she's utterly terrified. But trying to be very, very brave.

They continue to circle and circle, discuss and discuss. The beeping noise keeps beeping and beeping.

'But how the hell do I land, Steve? I don't even know how to slow down.'

One more circle above the town, keeping well clear of churches and tall chimneys, and they see the playing fields coming up ahead once more, the football and rugby pitches marked out in white. The hockey pitch, the running track. All those straight lines and curves as if a giant has leant down from the sky and traced them out on the grass.

Steve suggests they try landing there. It's completely flat and there's plenty of room. Grass, at least.

Fran says no. A really big no. 'If I try anywhere that's hard ground, I'll just crash us into it.'

Crash-landings. Steve's seen enough films to know

what happens – the explosion, the flames whooshing up to fill the screen, the ball of fire.

They could land in the river, maybe? If things go pear-shaped at least they'll have a chance to swim clear.

Best would be to land somewhere really soft. Steve suggests Robson's quarry, where there might be heaps of loose earth they could make for. Or else somewhere with lots of deep mud. Failing that, it's the river. Fran circles around a bit longer.

'I don't know – don't know – don't know.'

Steve wants to help her, show her he's with her. But she's totally tense, staring out of the windscreen as desperately as Nessie.

He taps her lightly on the arm.

They lurch down violently to the left.

'Don't touch me, Steve. I'm ready to explode.'

'Easy, Fran. I just want you to know we're together in this and we're going to get through it.' Even as he says the words he knows he sounds like a bad movie script.

'Thanks, Steve. We're together.' She turns to him for a split-second, gives him a taut smile. Then she goes and spoils it. 'And Dan too.'

 167

'Yes, Dan too.' What else can he say?

But she's gone rigid again, staring back out the windscreen.

'The river?' he suggests. 'Maybe it really is our best chance? With the doors already open, we can leap out the instant we hit the water. And we can all swim, even Nessie. Aim for a good long straight stretch and take it down as gradually as you can.'

'Oh yeah? Sounds easy.' She almost laughs, which makes them abruptly soar upwards. They steady again. 'I'd need a stretch a hundred miles long.'

'What about Baxter's Bog? It's flat, runs along next to the river and it's always oozy and muddy.'

'Yes! That's the one! Good call, Steve!' Then she stiffens. 'Oh God! Oh God! Oh God!'

He gives her arm a squeeze. He can feel the heat coming off her.

'Stay with me, Steve.'

'Not going anywhere. And if I did, I'd take you with me.' Bad film script again. 'We're going to land safely, Fran. We're going to make it.'

Fran touches the pedal to make them lurch to the left.

They complete a shaky half-circle and seconds later she calls out. 'There it is! Hold on, everyone!'

33

The beeping noise seems to have become more urgent, more frantic. Fran ignores it. Baxter's Bog is straight ahead, and approaching fast – a low-lying field with small streams running through it into the river, making the ground always slushy-soft with mud and puddles. Soft-ish, but not quicksand soft, much bigger than a football pitch, and covered with long grass, marshy bits and mud pools.

Fran leans forward and eases the lever to start gliding jerkily down. But the lower they go, the faster the ground seems to be rushing past beneath them. Faster and faster. The cockpit's shuddering, swaying from side to side. Beneath them the wet marsh, the tufts of grass, are coming closer and closer and ...

And before they know it, they've flown right over the bog, a metre too high.

'Going to turn and try again.'

Steve gives her arm a squeeze. Behind him, Dan's

making moaning-groaning-gulping noises. Steve hopes he's not going to throw up.

They lurch upwards again and Fran starts to steer round to the left once more to make her turn. They manage it in a series of jerks as she tap-tap-taps her foot on the pedal.

'Bloody thing!' she exclaims. 'Press too hard and we'll go into a spin. I can feel it.'

The turn is about completed when there's a sudden violent lurch, much worse than any so far. They drop several feet, then steady again. Then another lurch a couple of seconds later. The engine makes a coughing sound, then it coughs again, splutters, then catches. 'No! No!' Fran's almost in tears. 'That beeping . . .'

Steve had forgotten all about the beeping.

'It's not a built-up area warning at all,' she says.

Another cough-cough-cough from engine. Another lurch.

'It's telling us we're running out of fuel, that's what it is. All that standing around in the farm with the engine roaring away at full power.'

The engine catches again, then cuts out.

 171

Then catches again. They're losing speed, losing height, and fast. Far too fast.

Once again Baxter's Bog lies ahead of them, with pools of water glistening here and there between clumps of dark, soggy grass and mud. The helicopter's now dropping in a series of abrupt jerks, like they're falling down a set of stairs that keep disappearing beneath them and there's nothing to hold onto. The engine keeps stalling and threatening to stop for good every few seconds.

Suddenly it cuts out completely. The rotors start a loud rattle-clatter. Still travelling very fast, still a good couple of metres up in the air.

'Here we go, everyone! HOLD ON TIGHT!'

34

The ground's rushing towards them faster and faster. Tufts of grass rise up in front of them, they're almost touching the ground ... almost ... almost ... Then all at once *bump-bump-bumping* across – then *WHAM!* They skid, they slither-slide over sodden grass, over mud, splashing into brown marsh water that's thrown up over the windscreen. There's a screech, they're wrenched to one side. Too fast, too fast. The riverbank looms up ahead, then the river itself.

But they're slowing down ... slowing ... down ... down ... down. Starting to slew round in a long skid that goes on and on, everything drifting into slow motion.

Until ...

There's a final ...

Mega-JOLT!

They've stopped. Completely. Hardly a stone's throw short of the river.

Steve's hands are gripping Fran's and she's gripping his. Then, with one last shudder, the helicopter steadies, balances, and immediately begins slanting over to the left, tilting, starting to sink slowly, slowly into the sludge.

They've made it! Off with their headphones. Unbuckle, and onto their feet.

'YES! YES! YES!' High fives all round!

Steve opens the cockpit door. Nessie's first, with a giant four-paws-in-the-air leap to get onto solid ground where she stands and shake-shake-shakes herself to get all that noise, lurch, tremble and shudder out of her body. Steve clambers down only to go *SLAP!* into a soggy pool. Who cares? Quick as he can, he squelches round the front of the chopper to be ready to greet Fran. Standing there up to his ankles in mud, he reaches for her hand to help her down.

'You were fantastic!' he grins. '*FRAN*-TASTIC!'

Next moment, the three of them are hugging each other, jumping about in the mud and shouting, 'We did it! We did it!' at the tops of their voices. Nessie joins in, barking, wagging and splashing around in circles.

Fran's grinning from ear to ear. On a high – a mega-high. And so she should be.

Steve says it again: 'FRAN-FRAN-FRAN-TASTIC!' Which makes her laugh. He reaches forward to give her the biggest hug in the world ever, but his foot slips and he's almost splatted out full-length into the mud. Which makes her laugh again. Nessie's floundering around, her paws sinking deep into the boggy sludge, trying to jump herself clear, and all the time barking and barking and barking.

They can hardly believe it. They've landed! Landed, and they're still alive!

It takes them only a couple of seconds to splatter and splash to the edge of the bog and up onto the riverbank where Steve falls to his knees.

'Thank God, and thank Fran!' he cries out, then leans over and kisses the grass.

'The best big sister ever!' adds Dan.

They collapse on the ground. So, so glad.

No more lurching, no more swerving or being thrown about the sky. Just good solid *terra firma* that doesn't shift and slide around beneath them. Also, they're suddenly

aware how quiet it is. No more engine-roar, no more rotors whirling and screaming. It seems very still now. Peaceful.

For a moment the three of them sit in silence. Grinning at each other. Feeling good, feeling wonderful. Feeling totally stunned. Till they start laughing as they watch Nessie – she must be feeling as happy as them – roll around the grass, tumbling and somersaulting for sheer joy.

Then Mr Doom speaks up. 'What about the helicopter?'

'Who cares?' says Fran. 'It can sink into the bog and disappear forever as far as I'm concerned, and good riddance. Economy class from now on.' Then she adds, 'Or maybe business class?' She flourishes the plastic bag Kojak had put in the car. 'Let's see if he planned to cheat us.'

They gather round to peer inside . . . and can hardly believe their eyes. Banknotes, a big fat bundle of them.

'Wow!'

'We'll split it up later.' Fran slides the money up the front of her sweatshirt. 'Tell no one – and I mean *no one*.

You have to promise. Our parents would just waste it on fridges or leather couches or new kitchens. We'll hide it somewhere – and be set up for life!'

Steve and Dan both promise.

They're getting to their feet when they see someone coming along the bank towards them. Loads of people must have noticed them circling round and round the town. It's not every day you see a helicopter emergency-landing in a field. A woman who's a few metres ahead of the rest is leading a whole procession of welcome, it looks like. Behind her must be a dozen, twenty people at least. A real crowd come to greet them. They're famous!

It's Mrs Connor! No wind-up clockwork walk like her old man's, but skipping along like a spring lamb and waving both arms fit to burst. 'Yoo-hoo! Yoo-hoo!' Her face is an all-over smile. 'Yoo-hoo!'

She opens her arms wide and unfurls them for a big welcoming hug. 'Stevie! Stevie! Stevie! Am I glad to see you!'

Steve's pleased to see her, too. Of all the grown-ups, she's one of the best. But does he want to be hugged?

'Come here to me!'

So he goes. He gets himself hugged. Smothered, more like. She's a wrap-around bundle of brightly coloured scarves, and wearing a hat that's a tangle-trail of long wispy feathers.

'These are your friends?'

'This is Fran – she flew us and landed us.'

'Ah yes. Of course. Equality in the skies – and quite right too! Your dad has the garage, doesn't he, dear?'

'Yes.'

Mrs Connor taps her on the arm. 'Of course he does. Must've been useful for learning to fly. Now then, let's get you all home. Your parents have been so worried. Hardly slept a wink, I'll bet. Everyone in the whole town's been worried. Disappearing like that. And suddenly here you are! Surprise – out of the skies!' Then she sing-songs, 'You've been so far, you're spec-tac-u-lar!'

Word must have got round fast because more and more people are now coming along the path to see what's going on. They're celebrities! Like they're a famous band, or the royal family or something, the three of them stride through the crowd, smiling and waving at everyone. Nessie runs along the bank in front of them and then comes running back. Up and down she goes, grinning at them: *Come on, come on! We're home!*

Surprisingly, Mrs Connor is very good at leading the way and making sure they get clear of everyone. She's their security, their minder, going a few steps ahead like the bow of a ship, knocking people and their questions aside. If anyone does try stopping them, even for a moment, she's in there at once: 'Out of the way! Out the way! They need to rest and home's best!'

As they come onto the road she turns to Steve. 'Lucky I was passing and saw you land. Didn't know it was you, of course. Stopped the car for a good old nosey. And there you were! Amazing! Give them a lift home, I told myself. Back to the family bosom with them, I said. In you get.'

They pile into the Connor-mobile, Steve in the front with Nessie snuggled down at his feet, and FranDan in the back.

'Everybody comfortable?' Without waiting for a reply, or bothering to use her indicator, Mrs Connor pulls away from the verge, forcing a car coming along behind to brake and let her into the stream of traffic. She doesn't even notice. 'You'll be glad to get home, eh!'

'Yes, Mrs Connor, really glad.' *If we get there with you driving,* thinks Steve, and he holds onto Nessie for the comfort and security of them both.

Probably because she hardly ever looks at the road, Mrs Connor doesn't notice what a bad driver she is. She talks and talks, asking about the helicopter, telling them about how once she went parachuting, and always turning to Steve or, even worse, turning all the way round to FranDan in the back seat.

After five minutes' worth of sudden swerves, abrupt accelerations and slowdowns, of colour blindness at traffic lights and frequent hoots on the horn, they hear a police car speeding towards them from the other direction, siren blaring, blue lights flashing. For the first time, Mrs Connor seems aware there's actually someone else on the road apart from her and she stamps on the brake and swerves left into a quiet side street. She pulls in and parks. She watches in the rear mirror as the car zooms past the end of the street and continues in the direction of Baxter's Bog.

'Mrs Connor, why have you —?'

'That was the police, Steve, didn't you see them?

You don't want to speak to them *now*, do you? They're so nosey. All those questions and more questions, forms and more forms. You can do all that later when you're good and ready. Best to get you safe home first. Agreed?'

'Agreed.' Steve gives her his biggest smile. 'Smart thinking, Mrs Connor!'

Once the siren has faded into the distance, Mrs Connor starts up the car again and does a ten-point turn to get them facing in the right direction.

'First stop – home!' she calls out, and they jerk forward.

35

As they swerve into the street where they both live, Mrs Connor turns to Steve. 'We'll drop you off first. Afterwards it's straight on to Wilson's Garage for everyone in the back seat.'

Thank goodness. Only a few moments more and he'll be home. No more criminals, no more guns, no more helicopters and no more of Mrs Connor's driving – he'll see his mum and dad, he'll eat pizza, he'll sleep in his own bed . . .

Mrs Connor slaps her hand to her forehead. 'Silly, silly me! Silly-billy me!' She takes both hands off the steering wheel to straighten her hat – which sends the car nearly up onto the pavement. She hardly notices, just swerves back onto the road again. 'I just remembered. I saw your parents going into town, Steve, not twenty minutes ago. They told me they were going to the supermarket to get stocked up in case you suddenly appeared. Nice of them, don't you think?'

'Yes, that's very—'

She's stopped the car right in the middle of the street – the better to carry on their conversation. 'Wish I knew which store and I'd take you right there, but your mum never said. So here's what we'll do. You can wait in my house, Steve. And you two ...' She turns round to face FranDan. 'But, my goodness, now that I take a look at you, all muddy and marshy after that bog! Best come inside for a few minutes – that grungy gunge needs soap and sponge! Get you freshened up, then home in ten minutes. How does that sound?'

'Thank you, Mrs Connor.' Fran nods politely. 'Sounds great. You're very kind.'

The car moves forward another twenty metres then abruptly swerves to the left. Luckily the Connor front gate is open. They drive straight into the Connor garage – lucky the door's open, too – and get out. The garage connects directly with the house, something Steve's only seen in films. Cool.

'Come along, boys, come along, Fran, dear!' Mrs Connor opens the door. Nessie scampers straight into the house. 'All those muddy paws!' Mrs Connor shakes

her head and grins. 'Dogs will be doggies – can't help they're not moggies! In you go now.' She leads them along a wide corridor, still talking non-stop. 'You'll have a story, a real jackanory, to tell! But not till you're all cleaned up and ready. I'll make some tea, and there's choccy biscuits. I hope you like choccy biscuits?'

At the magic word, Nessie gives Mrs Connor all her attention – *Where are they? Can I have some?* – determined to stick close to her until the very last biscuit's been crunched up and swallowed. Mrs Connor opens the door at the end of the corridor and shows them into a large bathroom that's a full-on splash of rainbow colours swirling from floor to ceiling. 'Plenty hot water, plenty towels.' She pulls the door shut – and locks it.

Steve laughs. What's the old girl doing? Talk about being on another planet. He shakes his head and shouts to her through the door: 'Mrs Connor! Mrs Connor!'

Her voice comes singsong-ing back: 'Can't hear you! Can't hear you!'

He shouts louder, raps on the door. 'Mrs Connor, what're you doing? You've gone and locked us in and—'

'So I have! And silly me, I've lost the key!'

'You've – what? Come on, Mrs Connor, let us—'

'My husband said I was to keep you safe till he got home. Never said why. Or I can't remember. I'm such a scatter-brain, a runaway train, I'm off the tracks and on again.'

They hear her go pad-pad-padding away down the corridor, Nessie following.

Mr Clockwork Connor wants them locked up? Why on earth would he want that? Steve bangs his fist loudly on the door. No response. No Mrs Connor. She's just gone off and left them. They're stuck. A quick look round – no window to climb out of and the room's tiled solid.

'Off the tracks? She's off her trolley!' says Dan. 'She said she was going to take us home.'

Just then, classical music starts up somewhere in the house. Really loud and opera-sounding.

'We're locked in! We're prisoners!' shouts Dan.

'Not for long, Dan my man!' Steve raises his hand for silence and gives them both a big grin. At last, his big moment. 'I've got a key. A key to open every door in the world.'

185

36

Steve pulls out the gun. FranDan stare at him, in shock.

Further down the corridor, Mrs Connor has started to sing along with the music, screeching at the top of her voice. A runaway train, all right.

'Stand back.' Steve's seen it done a hundred times in films – the cop shoots out the lock and the door swings open. Easy-peasy. Never fails. But this isn't a film. It's a real lock, a real door – and he's holding a real gun.

He takes up a CSI stance with his legs apart. A moment to focus, concentrate. Then he points the barrel so it's right up against the keyhole, touching it. He won't miss at this range, not even him.

But . . .

His hand's started shaking. Shaking so bad that the tip of the barrel rattles against the lock. Next moment, Dan's standing beside him.

'Like they tell the rookie cops in the films, Steve,

breathe out slowly. Then, when you're ready, *squeeze* the trigger.'

'Yeah, right.'

He breathes out slowly and . . .

Magic! The trembling's almost gone. His finger curls around the trigger and—

Click!

Nothing. No big bang, no bust lock.

'Bloody useless!' he shouts.

'Shoot it again,' says Dan.

'Gun's not even loaded.' Steve's furious. He turns away, meaning to pull the trigger once more just to show them.

'No, Steve, no! You're going to—'

BANG!

The cabinet mirror shatters and the glass explodes, showering small pieces into the air and all over the bathroom. Fran and Dan scream and leap clear.

The gunshot blast still ringing in his ears, Steve stares in shock at the wrecked cabinet, at the broken glass littering the wash-hand basin and lying scattered everywhere on the floor. He's done all *that*?

'But it wasn't loaded. It wasn't. How could . . .?'

'Put it down.' Fran's voice is shaky, but she's really furious. 'You want to kill us?'

Managing to speak between taking big panic-gulps, Dan stammers out, 'Like in the films ... the first chamber's ... often kept empty ... for safety ... Kojak and Elvis were scared whenever it ... was pointed at them ... remember?'

Steve nods. 'Yeah. The gun works all right.' After a deep breath to calm himself, he turns to face the door again. Outside, the loud music has stopped.

'All that excitement ...' Mrs Connor comes back and calls through to them, 'and I forgot to ask for the gun you stole.'

'How do you know about that?' says Fran.

'My husband told me.'

'How did your husband know?'

'His friends told him, and they'll be here soon to say hello and get their stuff back.'

'What friends? What stuff? What are you on about?'

'Their gun, silly, and their money. By the way, you should be careful with that gun. Don't wreck my lovely bathroom. I spent weeks painting those tiles. Do you like them?'

'Do I – what? Who cares about your tiles.' Steve is lining up to take another shot at the lock.

'Anyway, all that noise you're making is frightening your poor doggie here.'

'Go away, Nessie! Go away!' he shouts.

'A sweet doggie she is, too. Loves her biscuits. Have you had her long?'

'Go away, Nessie! I can't shoot at the door when you're—'

'Kojak and Elvis are a nice pair of lads really. Had a hard life since coming out of the army, but they've picked themselves up and started their own business like the government tells people to do. They're ever so hard-working and—'

There's a ring at the doorbell.

'That'll be them now!'

With loud barks of welcome Nessie's gone rushing off down the corridor.

BANG! Steve shoots the lock. But the explosion makes the gun kick in his hand. He's missed, the bullet going a good couple of inches off target.

This time he rams it two-handed right up against the keyhole. Deep breath. Focus, concentrate. *BANG! BANG! BANG!*

There's nothing left of Mrs Connor's lock now. Not much left of her door, either. Too bad. He wrenches it open, angrier than he's ever been in his life. He feels like shooting them all – Mrs Runaway-train Connor, Kojak, Elvis. They're standing just inside the front door at the other end of the corridor. Part of him wants to blast the whole lot of them in one go, blast them to pieces. Them and their drugs and their greed and their—

'Hold it, kid. Calm down.' Kojak's coming towards him.

'Nessie, here! Biscuits! Biscuits!' Steve calls her. And at the magic words she comes rushing back up to him.

'Grab her, Fran. Hold her.' Raising the gun, he steps out into the corridor. 'Don't you come any nearer, Kojak!'

Kojak halts. 'Think you've got the only shooter in the world?' He reaches into his inside pocket.

Steve fires, but aiming wide enough to miss.

BANG!

The thug freezes, shocked.

Steve's shocked, too. He can hardly believe what he's just done and doesn't dare think what he might do next. His heart's hammering like mad.

37

Kojak's the first to recover.

'Take it easy, kid. We just want to talk, that's all. No reason for anyone to get hurt.' He takes a step closer.

'Stay where you are.'. Steve raises the gun again. He feels his hand shaking, worse than before. Behind him, Nessie's barking and barking.

Kojak is now midway along the corridor. 'We're reasonable people, Elvis and me. Don't want any trouble. We're businessmen.'

Businessmen? With his shaved head, biker denims, the fierce tattoos? Most of all, the threat of violence that comes off him like the worst smell ever.

'Don't listen to him.' Fran's standing beside him now. 'He's bad. Bad through and through.'

The thug gives them his broken-glass smile. 'If you don't watch out, Stevie boy, that young lady's going to rule your life. Ignore her. Let's keep this between you and me. Man to man.'

The shaking in his hand's getting worse. Steve takes a deep breath, then breathes out slowly. His hand steadies. The gun steadies.

'Leave Fran out of it.'

'Exactly what I'm saying – best if you and me just—'

Steve points the gun right at the thug. 'Turn around – you and Elvis. And out the door.'

Kojak makes a sucking noise through his teeth. 'Can't do that Stevie-boy. Too late now to—'

Next moment the thug's taken two quick steps forward.

Without thinking, Steve fires.

Kojak's stopped in his tracks, standing rigid in the middle of the corridor. Like he might topple over at any moment.

Steve stares, horrified. What happened? Has he shot him? Is the biker about to clutch his stomach or his heart or somewhere, and fall dead on the floor?

For a moment no one moves.

Then from the front door Elvis shouts down the corridor. 'All this shooting, the cops'll be showing up any minute. I'm out of here.'

Without turning round or taking his eyes off Steve, Kojak calls back. 'You leave now, Elvis, and you leave with nothing. No cut of the money, no drugs. No nothing. Don't worry about the plods – we'll hear them coming a mile off.'

Steve breathes out. He must have missed. Thank God.

Fran's beside him. 'There'll be no more warning shots. Right, Steve?'

CSI again: 'Copy that.' He gives the thug a hard stare. 'The next bullet's got your name on it, Kojak.'

He sees the man's eyes flicker uncertainly, sees him take a step back.

Steve moves towards him.

Kojak retreats another step. 'We *know* you. Steve and Fran. Well, let me tell you, Steve and Fran, it won't end here. We'll find out where you live. Easy done. And then one night we'll come and—'

'You forgot me. I'm Dan.' Dan's voice is shaking only a little as he steps forward. The three of them are now standing side by side, facing Kojak.

Then things start happening very quickly.

'BISCUITS!' shouts Elvis from the door.

Nessie breaks free of Dan and goes streaking down the corridor.

Steve rushes after her.

Kojak grabs hold of him. Gets an arm-lock round his waist.

Steve drops the gun. He's struggling to twist free. His legs at full-stretch, he's kicking wildly. Manages to big-toe the gun and send it clattering back along the floor towards Fran.

She picks it up. Points it at Kojak, who's now holding Steve in front of him like a shield.

'Steve was right, the next bullet's got your name on it.' Fran raises the gun.

'You'll hit your boyfriend here,' Kokjak shouts back.

Steve watches in horror as he sees Fran look down the raised barrel of the gun and take aim.

38

At the other end of the corridor Nessie has just discovered two new things –

First, there are no biscuits.

Second, she doesn't like Elvis. Doesn't like him at all. She doesn't really like either of the men – they'd kept trying to hit her with sticks, hadn't they? But one of them gave her meat. Lots and lots of meat. Kept feeding her. She likes being fed.

She heads back down the corridor to where the meat is. In the man's pocket.

'So, little girl, do you *want* to kill your boyfriend?' taunts Kojak.

Steve feels himself being lifted up until Fran's gun seems to be pointing straight at him.

'No killing kids,' shouts Elvis. 'I'm out of here.' A moment later the front door's slammed shut behind him.

'He's got no bottle.' Kojak spits on the floor. 'Same when he was in Afghanistan – always needing someone

196

to hold his hand. And you, Stevie boy, you got the bottle to get shot at?'

Steve stares up at Fran. He can see she's concentrating, eyes squeezed tight, trying to focus. Trying to keep her hand steady. 'Remember, Fran – deep breath,' he calls to her. 'Then let it out slow and ease back the trigger. And please don't miss.'

Each time Fran is about to fire, Kojak jerks Steve from side to side so she can't see where to aim without hitting him.

There's real scorn in her voice. 'You talk about folk having bottle, Kojak – and here's you hiding behind a kid,' she shouts. 'You're pathetic! A nobody with no hair and no bottle. You're a total coward, and you deserve everything you've got coming to you.' She aims again and is about to pull the trigger when …

… when Nessie jumps right in front.

She knows the meat is in the man's pocket. She can smell it. She can taste it almost. That delicious, sticky, chewy treat. Her paws are up on the man's shoulders. He's trying to push her away, trying to punch her out the road.

Steve sees his chance and when Nessie's distracting Kojak – who's only got one arm now to hold him – he leans forward and bites the back of the man's hand. Bites it hard.

The thug screams in pain, lets go, and scrambles to his feet. In the distance there's the sound of approaching sirens.

'Bloody dog, bloody kids, and now the bloody cops!' He turns and races up the corridor and out into the street.

'Goodbyeee!' Mrs Connor calls after him. She's shaking her head. 'Leaving the door wide open like that, you'd think he was born in a field.' She pulls it shut. 'Just as well he's gone, my dears, there's only enough choccy biscuits for the four of us.' She gives them a big smile. 'Tea for four – I'll go and pour!'

Steve turns to FranDan, who're now both beside him in the corridor, holding Nessie between them. 'Everyone all right? Because . . . because I don't think I am.'

He feels very woozy and dizzy all of a sudden. Next, the floor's starting to slip from under him. He's wanting to lean against the wall to keep himself upright, feeling worse than after one of those turning you upside-down-and-inside-out rides at a theme park.

Fran drops the gun so she can grab him to break his fall.

Even though he knows he's almost fainting, there's one last thing he's got to do. Doesn't know why, but he just *has* to.

He stares down at the gun lying on the floor. Then, using the very last of his strength, he kicks it as hard as he can the full length of the corridor, as far away from them all as possible. Wishing he could kick it out of sight forever.

'You've gone totally white, and—' Fran's holding him on one side and Dan on the other. His breath's coming in short gulps and gasps.

'Steve, we'd better get you through to the sitting room so you can—'

'Sit here … need to sit … down here.' Suddenly he feels so very heavy and so slack that, with FranDan still holding him, he slides down to the floor, his back slumped against the wall and his legs stretched out in front of him.

Fran's got her arm around him, steadying him. Nessie's all over him, whimpering and licking his face, while jumping from side to side at the same time. When Dan starts grinning at him, like he's trying to cheer him up, he looks so concerned and so really silly at the same time that all at once Steve bursts out laughing.

Mrs Connor appears, carrying a plate of biscuits. 'Well, well, well – everyone still here? So you fancy a corridor picnic instead, do you? What a great idea!' Which makes Steve laugh even harder – he can't stop.

Then Mrs Connor turns to Fran. 'Tea's ready and waiting, if you'd like to bring it through and be mother.' Her mobile rings. 'That'll be my husband.' She takes it out. 'Yes, dear?'

Fran sends Dan through for the tea. 'Steve needs plenty of sugar,' she calls after him.

'I picked them up as you asked, dear. And locked them in the bathroom like you told me. But then your friends arrived. There was some gun shooting. Real rooting-tooting gun shooting. Then your friends decided to leave.'

Steve can hear more police sirens now. Nessie's

nuzzling up, cold-nose and warm-tongue wet all at once. It feels wonderful. The sirens are suddenly really loud – the police car must have turned into the street. He doesn't feel quite so dizzy now, but doesn't let on. With Fran's arm around him, he'd be happy to stay sitting in the corridor like this for a few hours longer.

Mrs Connor puts away her mobile. 'I don't think my husband's coming back.' She starts handing round the biscuits.

Steve glances up in time to see two policemen come rushing in through the front door.

39

So glad to be home! thinks Steve. Seems years since he and Nessie slipped out of the house and ran through the midnight streets before setting off with FranDan down the river. Where's their raft now – in the middle of the Atlantic, halfway to America?

Whatever. He's glad he's not on it. Glad he's back with his mum and dad. Glad he's sitting on the floor sharing a special non-Tuesday late-night pizza with Nessie – everyone watching him and FranDan on TV. They've seen it three times already – it's been breaking news on BBC, ITV, Sky and now it's gone worldwide on BBC News 24. They're recording it to put it on YouTube later.

And here, for the fifth time on the screen, is them coming out of the Connor house. The old girl really is on another planet – probably from taking some of those drugs her husband was selling for Kojak. Mrs Connor is cool, even if she did keep them prisoner. Life on Planet Happy is all-day sunshine and kindness.

'Lock her up and throw away the key!' His dad shouts at the television. The TV ignores him, and so does Steve. The last couple of days have been a real learning curve and he's already tweeted some of what he's learnt:

Most adults act like they know everything, but they don't. Kids are often more grown up than most adults will ever be.

He helps himself to another slice of pizza. This is what life is really all about: a slice of pizza in each hand, one to share with Nessie, taking a bite each in turn, and the other piece all his.

Next up onscreen, the three of them are coming out the cop shop after 'helping the police with their enquiries'. Now they're standing between two detectives and two uniforms, about to get interviewed.

'Listen up – this is it! This is it!' he calls from the floor. His mum and dad stop eating. There's a respectful silence, a pause in the background pizza-chewing, can-slurping and beer-burping from the couch. He and Nessie don't stop gobbling the pizza, though – the taste of a celebratory double-cheese meat feast makes being on television even better.

The reporter's come up to them. He takes a quick look at his notes, then begins to speak.

'Here are Steve Merrick and Fran and Dan Wilson, the junior heroes of the day!'

Fran's straight in there. 'Less of the junior!' You can see the reporter nearly choking on his microphone.

'Fran's the goods, isn't she!' Steve calls out.

'Not very polite,' says his mum.

His dad belches – but it's the beer and not him, as he tells them for the zillionth time.

'Sssh! It's me next!'

'Well, Steve,' says the interviewer. 'You were captured by a desperate drug gang and held prisoner, but managed to escape in a *helicopter*, can that really be correct?'

'Sure is,' he tells the whole world, including Nessie, who's sitting up at full alert and almost blocking the screen. She doesn't get it – how can his voice come from the TV while at the same time he's sitting next to her? 'We stole it. Jumped in and took off. Fran did the controls and flew us back home. Travelled in style – helicopter posh class!'

'And, Ms Wilson ...' The interviewer turns to Fran, and you can see he's nervous already. 'Had you ever flown a helicopter before?'

'Have *you*?'

'Me? No.'

'Well, you should get out more!'

Steve punches the air. 'Nice one, Fran!'

Then she goes on. 'It was awesome, like being the lightest, the fastest, most wonderful butterfly ever, sweeping across the sky like we'd grown our own wings – it was pure magic!'

'There we have it, viewers. "Pure magic!" And now, Detective Osborne, what about the gang itself? What is the current status of the investigation?'

'We have one of the gang members in custody; he has been charged and is being questioned at this very moment. We found the farmhouse where the children were held. The gang were growing poppies to manufacture heroin. We are following up a number of promising leads. A local drug dealer, Mr Connor, whom we've had our eye on for some time, has also disappeared. However, we are confident that...'

The news item finished, his dad zaps it over to *Britain's Got Talent* and is fart-snoring within minutes.

Steve and Nessie polish off the last of the pizza between them. Suddenly he feels totally knackered. Like he can hardly move.

Climbing upstairs to his room an hour later upgrades him to super-knackered. Too knackered to get into bed even. Nessie's come with him, but she's so full of pizza and adventures that she stretches out on the floor and immediately falls fast asleep, her legs kicking like she's running after a whole packet of salami.

He boots up the desktop. Zillion to the power zillion messages on Facebook. The whole world has seen them on TV. He posts to FranDan: *You two are the best. See u soon.*

Then he types out a private message, to Fran only: *You're the best and then some x*

He takes out the *x*, then changes his mind and puts it back in, then takes it out again. He does this half a dozen times. Finally he makes it *xx*, and sends it.

There's an endless two-day-long barf-strand from dickhead Thor and his dickhead Vikings. Sometimes he'd been posting every few minutes, like he couldn't help himself, and not getting any response from him and Dan had made him more and more frantic.

Wish you were dead . . . Why don't you top yourselves . . . You're both gay . . . and all the rest of it. Same old, same old . . . What a load of pathetic, whining drivel.

He scrolls down to Thor's most recent puke-post: *Think youre big now youve been in a plane? Well youre not. Big sister had to drive you home. Better if she crashed you, better if you all . . .*

He doesn't read the rest. Under his breath he whispers, 'Come tomorrow, you're toast, whoever you are.'

With a single mouse click he deletes the lot.

After a last goodnight pat to Nessie, who gives him back a gentle snore, Steve switches off his light and snuggles down under the duvet. It's so great to be back in his own bed. He's no sooner closed his eyes than he finds himself imagining he's on the raft again, tramping up the hill with all their stuff, finding the cave, the kitbag, Kojak, Elvis, the farm, the helicopter, the shoot-out at Mrs Connor's, then seeing himself and FranDan on TV. . .

What an amazing time they've had, the three of

them! They've only taken on a whole gang, an *armed* gang, and smashed it! Kojak's in jail and the rest of them are on the run. Fran even made sure she brought back their £15,000 secret cash bonus – all theirs and no one else knows! Fran is the best.

Raising both hands above his head, he high-fives himself. 'Yes!'

Which leaves dickhead Thor and his dickhead Vikings at the top of his Things To Do list for tomorrow. He can hardly wait!

40

When Steve wakes up next morning, Bart Simpson's arms are stretched open wide to greet the new day and show him it's already nine-fifteen. Everyone's at school and he's still in bed! Good or what? Outside, not a cloud in the sky and the sun shining full blast. Even better – he can smell bacon, he can smell toast. Better and better and best – no rafts, no caves and no criminals.

He jumps out of bed. Next stop – breakfast!

But first a quick text to FranDan.

Yesterday, Kojak – today, Thor. See u at school. After break.

He comes out the shower to find Dan's texted back.

Let's do it!

His mum grins at him as he enters the kitchen. 'The three of you were on TV again this morning and you're all over the front page. The paper's next to your plate.'

The headlines take up half the page: *KID HEROES TAKE ON DRUG GANG!*

There's a photo of the three of them outside the police station – and they're looking pretty good! A smaller photo at the bottom shows the helicopter tilted to one side and partly sunk into Baxter's Bog. Steve gazes at it ... and gazes at it ... and gazes at it. That's *them*! That's really them!

His mum's still talking. 'Imagine Fran flying that helicopter, and her such a slip of a girl. Here you go.'

A full plate, and then some. He starts in with the fork and knife.

'Pretty girl, too,' she adds.

He gives a bacon-sounding grunt he hopes could mean anything.

'No one's expecting you to go to school today, Steve.' His mum's now second-helping him with more bacon and another fried egg to keep it company. 'After what you've been through these last few days you need to rest, you need to take it easy and ...'

He stops listening. Grown-ups are always saying they need to rest and take it easy. No wonder the world's in such a mess with all the good people sitting around resting and taking it easy, leaving the bad ones like Kojak and Elvis free to do whatever they want – make drugs, drop bombs, turn little kids into migrants, kill off seals and elephants . . .

He stacks up three slices of bacon and slots them in place for a triple-layer toast sandwich, which he chews and chews and chews while his mum talks and talks and talks. Finally they're both finished.

'Thanks, Mum.'

He stands up. Time to go. Time to sort out Thor.

The three of them meet in the street outside the school gates. Through the railings they can see the playground's empty except for the janitor leaning on his brush over by the side door.

Everyone's in class. Good.

After an enthusiastic catch-up about seeing themselves on TV last night and making the front pages this morning, they high-five each other.

'This is the day Thor gets what's coming to him,' announces Steve.

'Yeah.' Dan slips into his best movie-speak drawl. 'We'll punch his ticket good!'

Fran pushes open the school gates and they go in.

At once, Dan's back to being the usual Dan. 'But we still don't know who Thor is.'

'We will.'

'How?'

Good question for once. Steve doesn't know the answer. Nobody does. Here they are, wired up, ready to go for it, ready to rock, ready to kick ass! Only, where do they start?

'The class,' says Steve. 'He must be someone in our class, and his Vikings, too.'

'Or *she* must be,' says Fran.

Steve's about to say that girls aren't rough and don't cause trouble, when he remembers Fran forcing Kojak to back down as she ripped open packet after packet of drugs; and how, at Mrs Conner's, she might even have shot Kojak if he'd not been in the way.

'OK, you're right. Thor could be a girl. It's possible.' Though he still didn't believe it, not really. 'Let's just go into class and we'll take it from there.'

Dan punches the air. 'Bring it on!'

212

They ring the security bell at the main door, and say their names into the intercom.

'Oh, it's *you*!' It's Mrs Chalmers, who runs the school office, and she sounds really excited. 'Come in! Come in!'

The door buzzes open.

Mrs Chalmers has rushed into the corridor to greet them and fuss over them about how brave they are and how everyone's seen them on TV and all over the papers and . . .

Then Mr Anderson, the headmaster, appears. He's a tall man and bends down to shake hands with each of them in turn, saying about them being brave and on TV and all over the papers and how the school is really proud of them and . . . and . . . and . . .

Steve's getting more and more impatient. He's so pumped up wanting to sort out Thor that the energy's zapping around inside him. He can hardly stand still and might explode at any minute.

Fran must be feeling the same because the instant the headmaster pauses for breath, she says, 'Thank you, Mr Anderson, that's really nice of you, but we'd better get going to our class. We've missed a few days and want to catch up with things as soon as possible.'

The headmaster beams down at them. 'Of course, of course. Most commendable. You run along, the three of you. This afternoon we'll have a special school assembly to welcome you back and for everyone to show how proud they are of you.' Mr Anderson hardly looks like a headmaster any more, more like a big grin on stilts.

They set off down the corridor.

Dan's clearly pumped up too. 'Right then, so what are we going to do?'

No answer.

Dan rushes a couple of steps ahead, then turns to face them.

'Steve? Fran? What are we going to do?'

'Stay cool, little brother.'

'I can't. I can't. I've got to do – something. Something!'

At the end of the corridor they reach the class door. Then come to a stop.

From inside, they hear Mrs Dawson talking about

maths – which Steve has missed like a hole in the head – and through the glass panel they can see her pointing at the whiteboard and explaining stuff and more stuff while the class sit at their tables, writing it all down.

Before they have a chance to work out how they're going to play it, too-many-movies Dan says, 'Let's do this thing!', then opens the door and walks straight in.

'If we multiply using—'

Mrs Dawson stops in mid-sentence.

'Fran! Dan! Steve! We weren't expecting to see you till next week – not after all those adventures you've been having. It's great you're here!' She turns to the class. 'Let's give our heroes a warm welcome.' She starts clapping and the class join in, some of them whistling and whooping.

As if he's watching it on TV, Steve mutes the sound for full concentration. There are twenty-eight in the class, spread over six tables. Though he looks like he's doing nothing but accepting their applause, he lets his gaze pass from face to face, Half-Pint, Big Robo and the rest, scanning each of them in turn. He's not sure what he's scanning for, maybe a shifty look in someone's eyes, maybe a smile that might just be pretend. Whatever. He's scanning to see what doesn't feel right.

The applause finishes. He's scanned everyone . . . and seen nothing.

41

By lunchtime they still have no idea who Thor is, or how to find out. Fran had hoped one of the girls at her table might have heard something. But no, not a thing.

The bell goes and everyone rushes out the door, down the corridor and out into the playground. Within seconds the whole school, it seems, are clustered round FranDan and Steve, wanting to hear about everything.

The three of them have to clamber up onto one of the benches and, like it's a press conference on TV, they take questions.

What were the drug dealers like?

Were they like in the films?

Did they all have guns?

Did they shoot them?

What was it like firing the gun?

What was the woman in the gang like? What was she wearing?

Was she as bad as the men?

What was it like flying the helicopter?

Were they scared?

What about Nessie?

Then someone asks, 'Can I have your autographs?'

Then someone else says, 'Me too!'

'Me, too!'

And suddenly they're getting rushed by everyone in the playground, all waving bits of paper and pens into their faces. A tsunami of kids washing over Bench Island and nearly drowning them.

The bell rings and they're still signing.

And that's when Steve notices Half-Pint Pete standing by himself at the back of the crowd, and looking like a sad little elf. As usual, he's hanging around the edge of things without really taking part.

Suspicious?

OK, so he doesn't fit – but, really, could *he* be Thor? Not in a million years. He's just Half-Pint, he's nothing.

Once the tsunami has rolled back enough to let them climb down from the bench, they start towards the main school door and Steve feels someone tug at his T-shirt. It's the sad little elf.

'Really glad you're all right and everything.'

'Thanks, Pete.'

Everyone's streaming back into the school, but the instant FranDan and Steve arrive at the door, the crowd stands aside to let them go first.

'Like we've won the X Factor!' says Dan. Just then a small boy darts up to tap him on the arm. Rushing back to his pals, he shouts, 'I touched Dan! I touched Dan!'

Dan's grinning. 'We'll need minders soon!'

'Not us. We can take care of ourselves, no problem!' says Steve, but he can't help grinning back. 'See you in class.'

He pushes open the door of the boys' toilets and goes in. He doesn't really need a pee, but after all that clamour and attention, he wants to have a few minutes to himself.

He's just finishing when he realises that someone else has come into the toilets. But they're not coming over to the stalls or to the cubicles. They must be still over at the sinks. They've come in to have a wash? But they've not turned on a tap; there's no sound of water running. Are they wanting to see him? In private?

Steve turns round.

219

It's the sad little elf Half-Pint again. Christ, is this guy planning to follow him round forever like some kind of junior stalker? He runs the tap, squirts some soap, rinses, shakes off the water, uses the drier – and still nothing from the little elf. Doesn't speak, doesn't move. Just stands there.

When Steve goes to leave, the elf takes a step back, though he's not even in the way. He's about to pull open the door when the elf finally speaks up.

'I hear you've been asking around about Thor. When you find out who he is, will you batter him?'

Steve lets go of the handle and turns to face the elf. 'What's it to you?'

'Give him a real doing over, will you?'

'You're not Thor. You can't be!'

A look of fear crosses the elf face. 'No, not me. No way. If someone said I was, they're lying.'

Steve shrugs. There's something about Half-Pint that almost makes him want to stomp on him. Not that he ever would, of course, but still . . .

He's about to leave when—

'If I tell you something, do you promise not to batter me?'

Steve stops, turns round. 'What's that?'

The little elf looks down at the floor as if he's speaking to his feet, then says his next words really slowly. 'I'll tell you something – something you really want to know – but you've got to promise not to batter me.'

'If you know something, tell me.'

'You've got to promise.'

'You know who Thor is?'

'Promise!'

Without waiting, the elf looks up at him and there's almost a touch of pride in his voice as he says, 'I was his Vikings – all of them.'

'You?' Steve takes an abrupt step forward.

The little elf jerks back a couple of paces until he's right up against the line of sinks.

'You can't hit me. You promised.'

'It was you who posted all that stuff?' says Steve. 'But why? What did Dan and me ever do to you?'

The little elf stares back down at the floor and begins talking to his feet again. 'He said he'd batter me if I didn't. Said he'd post that I was gay, too.' A pause. 'And I'm not.

I don't know anything about it, about being gay. Or being anything.'

'Wouldn't matter if you were gay,' says Steve. 'It wouldn't matter at all.'

Half-Pint shrugs.

Steve takes a deep breath. He should walk away. Walk away right now. Walk away before he does something he'll regret.

But he doesn't.

After a longer pause, the elf looks up. 'Now you're going to batter me, aren't you?'

Too right he is. The sad little elf deserves to get thumped. It'd be a kindness really – a steep learning curve that he won't forget in a hurry. Steve's aware of his fists starting to clench. One part of him really wants to let fly. He can already feel how good it would be.

Thump – for telling him to top himself.

Thump – for telling Dan to top himself.

Thump-thump – for telling them both to top themselves.

Thump-thump-thump – for being all the Vikings.

But another part of him doesn't. Steve can see the sad

little elf will always be a sad little elf, all bony-thin and whining; he'll always get thumped. And he'll never, never, never learn.

So what's the point?

In fact, this part of Steve doesn't even want to touch him. It feels sorry for him. But not too sorry.

He prods his finger hard into the sad little elf's chest. 'Just stay out of our way from now on. Meaning forever.'

As he turns to leave, Steve catches the ghost of a smirk flit across Half-Pint's face – like not getting thumped means he's got away with it, and that's all that matters. For a split-second Steve feels like reconsidering things.

But he stops himself at the last moment. It would bring *him* down to Half-Pint's level – and he's better than that. So he just goes 'BOO!' making the elf leap his own height in the air. Then he says, 'You tell me who Thor is and we'll see what happens.'

For an instant Steve thinks the elf is maybe too scared that he'll get himself into more trouble – but then a look of craftiness, eagerness almost, flits across the small face.

'You'll give him a real doing over?' There's real relish as Half-Pint says the words.

'Who is it?'

'You will, though, like you did the drug dealers? And give him one from me.' His puny elf fist punches his puny elf palm. 'Make it your hardest.'

'Thor'll get what's coming to him. Who is he?'

The little elf puffs out his chest. 'Everybody saw the stuff on Facebook, but I'm the only person who—'

The door opens.

'Hey, Mrs Dawson's wondering where you've got to. I was sent to hurry you along.' It's Pizza McBride, a big boy – big as in round. Pizza-round.

'We're just coming,' says Steve.

'Oh, you're fine, Steve. You can come and go as you want, the school's all yours. But Half-Pint here needs to scoot himself along to class ASAP, or he's in trouble. Right, Pete? Get moving. I'll chum you back.'

The sad little elf shoots through the door double-fast. Pizza holds it open long enough for Steve to step past, then hurries on ahead to catch up with the elf and herd him safely along the corridor.

Back in the classroom, Steve finds Mrs Dawson in full maths mode, her whiteboard a multi-coloured tangle of numbers, plus, minus and equals signs, a swirl of arrows and underlinings. He takes his seat next to Dan.

When Mrs Dawson's turned her back to the class to add even more numbers and swirls to the tangle, he takes out his mobile. Under the table he texts Fran.

Might no who Thor is. Tell u at lunch.

He nudges Dan and shows him what he's sent.

'Who is it?' Dan says out loud, as if smartphones had never been invented.

Later.

42

By the time Steve gets out of class at lunchbreak, Half-Pint has already vanished. He hunts for him up and down the corridors, the lunch hall, the main hall, the toilets, the playground. No Half-Pint. If only Pizza hadn't shown up at the very moment the elf had been about to tell him who Thor was.

He gives up and texts FranDan.

Vic park. Now.

Victoria Park is at the end of the street; it's small and far enough away from the autograph hunters and the rest of their fans to give them a few minutes' peace.

The three of them meet next to the oak tree in the centre. Steve's been thinking.

'Better that I don't tell you the name. I might be wrong – it's just a guess. Not even that, a hunch really.'

'Who is it?' says Dan, as if Steve hadn't said a word.

He shakes his head. 'Not saying till after I've dealt with him.'

'Why not? You can tell me and Fran.'

'If I deal with him and it turns out it's not Thor, there'll be even more trouble.'

'But you can tell me,' says Dan. 'I'll help you. I'll put the squeeze on him and—'

'You will not,' says Fran. Firmly.

'Oh.'

She continues, 'And what about his Vikings, Steve? You can't take them on as well.' She looks concerned.

'The Vikings are already sorted. Turns out there was only one of them and he's nothing. I've dealt with him already. Only Thor himself now.'

'You're really going to do the whole heavy macho bit?'

'Certainly am.' Steve nods. Fran's bound to be impressed.

'Give him his teeth to play with? Make it so he'll need carried home?'

'Too right.' Another nod.

'All that thug stuff?'

Thug stuff? Is that what she thinks it is? 'I'll be giving Thor what he's got coming.'

'Then you'll get arrested and locked up.'

'I don't care.'

'Well, I do,' says Fran. 'I don't want to spend my evenings and weekends coming to visit you in prison.'

Would she really do that? Steve feels a rush of pleasure – of pride, even. Would Fran really come and visit—

Then she goes and spoils it.

'Nor does Dan.' She glares at her brother and prods him. 'Does he?'

'Eh?' says Dan. 'Oh. No, he doesn't. I mean – no, I don't.'

Fran turns back to Steve. 'Right then – no knocking out anybody's teeth, no macho muscle stuff. I have a much better idea.'

And she tells him.

'That's genius, Fran!' cries Steve. He wants to give her a big, big hug and maybe even a big, big kiss – but manages to hold back, not being sure how she'd respond. Instead, he says again, 'Genius. FRAN-TASTIC!'

43

'Today, boys and girls, is a very special day for us all. As we can see from the TV and press, the whole country has now heard of our school. For this we have to thank the courage and bravery of three of our most popular pupils. The twins Fran and Dan Wilson, and Steve Merrick.'

Loud cheers.

'Drugs are one of the biggest scourges of our time and often young people like yourselves are targeted by evil men. Sometimes the police seem helpless, but Fran, Dan and Steve have shown them what to do and how to do it. The criminals met their match. It seems that . . .'

They're on the stage of the main hall in front of the whole school. It's the special assembly, in their honour. Like Mr Anderson had told them in the morning, the whole school is present. The headmaster, being a headmaster, is giving a speech that seems to go on and on. He can't help himself – it comes with the job.

FranDan and Steve don't care. Though they're

standing next to Mr Anderson, they're so charged up with what they hope will happen next that their feet are hardly touching the platform. Steve feels like he's zooming through the air, hurtling backwards and forwards above the heads of the crowd gathered in the hall like a heat-seeking missile that's about to lock on target.

Finally, the booming sound of Mr Anderson's microphone voice falls silent. There's a huge burst of applause. Everyone's staring up at them, clapping, cheering and stamping the floor. It's like the wildest concert ever. They're stars! Megastars!

But the best is still to come.

When the applause dies down and Fran sees that Mr Anderson is about to tell everyone to return to their classes, she steps forward. Raises her hand for attention.

'Thank you, Mr Anderson, and thank you everyone. This really means a lot to us.'

More clapping, more cheering, more stamping.

Then Steve steps forward and raises his hand for silence. Realising he's been left behind, Dan steps forward, too.

Steve turns to the headmaster. 'We would like to take

this opportunity to publicly acknowledge and show our appreciation to the one person who made our adventure possible. The one person who inspired us to set out on our journey in the first place.'

Mr Anderson straightens his tie, ready to step forward just in case they mean him. Mrs Dawson looks puzzled – could Steve possibly mean her, their class teacher?

Fran takes over. 'Yes, this person deserves all the credit and deserves to be known to everyone.'

Then it's Dan's turn. 'Without them, without this person, I mean, we would never have … hmm … never have … never have gone away.'

Fran holds up her hand again. 'But no applause, please. This person is so shy. So very, VERY shy that they never use their real name. When they tweet or post on Facebook they call themselves—'

Suddenly there's a disturbance at the front of the hall, near the right-hand side. Everybody looks across in that direction to see a boy edging closer to the aisle like he's trying to sneak away. Next moment, he's been grabbed and is being held firmly by two of Steve's friends, who'd been tipped off in advance that something like this might happen. Steve's hunch had been spot on, but Fran had nailed it.

Steve makes the big announcement. 'Yes! There he is! Even now he's trying to avoid the limelight. Bring him up here for everyone to see. Bring him up so we can all have a good look at Thor – Thor the cyber-bully!'

As the boy is frogmarched towards the short flight of wooden steps leading up to the stage, Mr Anderson moves into full headmaster-mode. 'What's going on? What's all this about "Thor"? Why wasn't I informed? Why did no one think to tell me about this?'

FranDan and Steve ignore him and prepare to greet mighty Thor.

But Pizza McBride is having none of it. Despite the fact that he's about to be celebrated by the entire school, he's dragging his feet every step of the way, yelling at his captors. 'Let me go! I don't know anything about Facebook. I don't know anything about Thor. I don't know anything about anything.' His normally pasty-pale face has turned tomato-red, a defiant tomato.

Steve calls down to him, 'So why were you running away?'

'I wasn't feeling well.'

'You're going to feel a lot worse very soon.'

A loud cheer goes up from the hall.

Still shouting and yelling, McBride is pulled onto the stage. 'I'll sue you, sue the lot of you. I'll sue the whole school. My dad knows someone who will—'

He's hauled over to where FranDan and Steve are waiting for him. 'Shut it, Thor.'

McBride shuts it.

Steve steps up to the microphone. 'Meet Thor, everyone. Thor is the cyber-bully who tried to make Dan's life a misery, and then mine. This is what a coward and a bully looks like – a big fat nothing!'

'I'll get you for this!'

'Too late, Thor. We've got *you!*'

Again McBride falls silent. This time for good.

Mr Anderson tries to speak. 'Really, this is all most irregular. If you all come to my office, I will—'

Suddenly Steve sees that there are silent tears running down McBride's fat cheeks. And just as when he stopped himself from laying into the sad little elf, because he was such a pathetic little elf, he now wants to stop laying into

Pizza. The bully's been exposed and totally humiliated. Enough.

But not so Fran. She steps forward and takes over the microphone.

44

'Crying's not going to get you anywhere, Pizza,' announces Fran. 'We want an apology, a public apology – to my brother, Dan, to Steve.' She turns and gives Steve a smile that warms him from top to toe. 'And to all of us for bringing such cruelty and misery into our school.'

Steve is seriously impressed. If he had been in danger before of falling for Fran, the danger level's just been upgraded to IMMINENT.

No response from McBride. He's silent. An overripe tomato that's finally burst.

Fran continues. 'We can get the police, we can have you in court. We can see you're sent to prison.'

Not a word from Pizza McBride. Nothing.

'We can and, believe me, we will. This is your last chance. Step up to the microphone and say you're sorry. Say sorry to Dan, sorry to Steve and sorry to the whole school. Afterwards, that's it. Finished. What's said in the school stays in the school.'

There are nearly four hundred kids in the hall, plus the teachers, the admin staff, the janitor and his team, the kitchen ladies and even the lollipop man. A crowded hall, but after Fran's finished speaking, everyone is silent. It's a totally pin-dropping silence. Everyone's looking at McBride.

Finally he starts towards the microphone.

45

FranDan and Steve are walking across the school playground after the special assembly. In honour of their heroic deeds, Mr Anderson has given the whole school the rest of the afternoon off.

'Pizza McBride – what a total wimp!' says Steve.

'Do you think he really fainted or was he just putting it on?' asks Dan.

Fran shrugs. 'Who cares? We showed him up for what he was and, true to form, he bottled it at the last minute. All that matters is that everybody knows he was Thor and—'

Dan butts in: 'And he knows everybody knows, and everybody knows he knows that everybody—'

'Thank you, Dan.' Steve gives him a pat on the shoulder. 'We get the idea.'

They're passing through the school gates when Steve feels someone tug at his T-shirt. It's the sad little elf, yet again. He's about to tell him to stop following him everywhere and get a life when the elf speaks up. He's an angry little elf this time.

'You said you'd batter him and batter him good.'

'I said Thor'd get what was coming to him – and so will you if you don't shove off.'

'I told you to give him one from me, thump him your biggest.' Again the puny elf fist strikes the puny elf palm.

Steve looks down at the metre's worth of bad news. He shakes his head. 'Well, I guess I can't please everyone. Have a nice day!'

With Fran walking between the two boys, taking an arm each, they leave the school and head out to enjoy their afternoon of freedom. 'So, what's next?' she asks.

ACKNOWLEDGEMENTS

The author would like to thank his agent, Lucy Jukes, as well as Darcey Hundleby, Christian Staub, Lynda Clark and Pam Thomson for their helpful suggestions. And, most of all, an extra big thank you to his wife, Regi Claire, for her insightful criticism and enthusiasm.

Nessie would like to give Leila and Daisy many grateful wags – their friendship helped sustain her through this most perilous adventure.